TALK TO ME

by

Florence Witkop

CHAPTER 1

I was in no hurry. Maybe I should have been. If I'd been in a rush to outfit myself with new rain boots because my old ones had holes in them and rain was in the forecast and I'd driven straight to the city to get those boots instead of stopping to enjoy the view – well, if that had been the case, then none of it would have happened. But it was morning, and I had all day, so I decided to stop on the way.

Even so, if the strange wind hadn't chosen that moment to come up the canyon, then there'd still have been no problem. But it came, and there was nothing I could do about it except try to survive.

I'd turned off the highway into the familiar rest area with an overlook so gorgeous that whenever I had the time I stopped, and every time I was there, at the overlook, it took my breath away. Every. Single. Time.

The overlook jutted out over a long, deep but narrow valley of pristine wilderness intertwined with the tributaries of a whitewater river that dropped to the valley floor over a series of waterfalls that shot white foam against a green forest backdrop. It was at the top of a funnel formed by the valley that always sent at least a breeze from the bottom to the overlook. Sometimes a strong wind, but even on hot days with no wind at all, that overlook was comfortable. Cool and delightful.

The only thing in the valley not created by nature was some kind of building at the bottom, but it had been well designed and was a color that blended with the surrounding flora. Most people didn't even notice it, and the only reason I did was because I lived not far away and had been contacted by protesters trying to prevent it from being built.

I'd not cared one way or another as long as it didn't interfere with my enjoyment of the area, and the builders had been very careful about that, though I did end up on the protest group's hate list for not caring enough about what they considered a desecration of nature. Besides, they'd said, no one knew what that building would be used for. Their expressions had been ominous.

I'd laughed after they left because all I cared about was whether the view was still gorgeous after the building was erected. And it was. I stopped every chance I got, and that day was no exception.

Once parked, I headed for the well-marked path to the overlook. It was a rather long path and went upwards at a steep enough angle to leave me breathless when I arrived, but the view was worth it, and I always stayed long enough to catch my breath before the return walk.

That day there was someone else already there if

the ancient, dented pickup truck in the parking lot when I arrived belonged to a fellow lover of overlooks. It was old, really old, and I expected to find an equally old person at the end of the trail.

Instead, I saw a man several years older than me with the look about him that current and former military types can't seem to avoid. The posture. The bearing. The short hair. So it wasn't an elderly man. Instead, it was most likely a man who liked antique vehicles and hadn't gotten around to restoring his but was using it for transportation until he got around to doing the actual work.

I checked him out further. He was definitely military, from the top of his super short haircut to the bottom of his neat, shining shoes. He'd been blessed with an excellent physique that now held ramrod posture, and he had a calculating way of looking at everything and everyone, including me, as I joined him at the railing. But neither of us spoke. Until the silence grew awkward and I said, "Beautiful, isn't it?"

He nodded. Encouraged, I continued. "I love to stop here when I'm going somewhere. Anywhere." I took a breath and continued because he seemed to be listening though he didn't move and barely acknowledged my presence. "You'd think I'd get tired of the view, especially since I'm local and drive by here frequently. But I never do."

"It's awesome." Said without turning from the forest spreading below like a carpet of a thousand different shades of green. But he did answer. He did know I existed.

So I decided to continue and be friendly. "Are you local too?"

"Just passing through," he replied, finally turning enough to acknowledge my existence. Then he turned back to the view.

But instead of simply enjoying the view once more, he stiffened. Stared. Swore under his breath. And stared some more. "What the -- ?"

He leaned over the railing to see better, and he wasn't smiling. That trim body was suddenly tense, and his hands gripped the railing so hard they turned white. I looked to see what had caught his attention.

What I saw was totally wrong. It was terrifying. Life altering. Impossible. And real.

I tried to scream but I couldn't make a sound. It was horrible. And it shouldn't be there. Shouldn't exist. But it did exist and was slowly, inexorably filling the valley with pure horror.

I couldn't breathe. I could only watch as a wind, roiling and many-colored and sparking with electricity, came up the funnel formed by the valley. It was headed straight towards us. No, not just a wind, it was more than a wind, I could see that. It was composed of putrid clouds that billowed and turned in a tornado-like roll and was filled with fire sparking deep in it, and the whole mess grew exponentially larger and still larger as it rose along the valley.

It came up the hill slowly but deliberately.

And it was headed straight for us.

There were vortices rotating inside the multi-colored cloud and those vortices began turning, slowly at first but then faster and still faster as the whole thing rose inexorably up the hill, growing more frightening and gaining speed as it came, even as the sparking grew until the entire cloud was a mass of fireworks.

The closer it got the better we could see the details. The roiling mini-vortices. The horrendous colors. The electrical discharges. The uprooted brush and entire trees that had been torn out of the ground and were circling in the approaching vortex.

Towards us.

I could do nothing. I was frozen to the spot. Not so the military type. "Run!" he yelled as he moved even before I had time to react to the horror coming our way and think what to do.

But in the seconds since sighting the approaching cloud he'd somehow managed to turn, look over the area in that way he had that saw everything and, in less time than I could possibly see half of it, had assessed the entirety of the overlook and found the only safe place.

He pointed. He yelled again, knowing I wasn't in possession of my wits. "Between those rocks! It's our only chance!"

Without waiting for permission, he grabbed my hand and hauled me towards the rocks, running at top speed with his entire concentration on reaching those rocks. His thoughts didn't include me. I was incidental, a person who happened to be nearby when the world went crazy, and he dragged me along automatically.

I was familiar with the rocks we were headed towards. There were two of them, each twenty feet high at least with a narrow space between them that would provide the only safety in the overlook. I'd always thought of them as places for couples to make out. Now they were the difference between life and death.

Somehow I regained control of my body and got my feet beneath me and ran without being dragged. We both ran flat out. He jerked me ahead of him and I was fairly thrown between the rocks and slammed against one of them as the military type slammed against me.

I hugged the bare rock as hard as possible, making myself as small as I could while he spread his arms wide on either side of me, his front to my back, protecting me against what was coming as he tried to push both his body and mine into that solid rock.

Then the wind hit.

It was a living, breathing thing. It was both sound and fury and it howled with a sound that would have taken my breath away if I'd not already been holding it in sheer terror. It screamed like a banshee as those strangely colored clouds poured over the railing we'd been leaning against moments earlier, and it was full of currents that ebbed and twisted like monsters from hell. If we'd still been there, we'd not have survived.

The wind blew over and around the rocks we hid between and tried to penetrate between them, but they were solid, and no wind was a match for them. All that touched us was the cloud itself, diffusing and spreading out between the rocks with strange colors and electrical charges. We were soon immersed in a multi-colored fog. Sparks flashed everywhere, pushed by that wind from hell. But the rocks kept the wind itself at bay.

We lived. But we didn't survive unscathed. Something happened as that vile air surrounded us. As it filled the space between the rocks around us and pressed against our bodies.

It passed through our clothes and into our bodies. Then it moved through one of us and from that one to the other of us and then back again. From inside the man behind me to inside me and then in the reverse, from me back to him. Over and over again, in and out of us both, taking from me and giving to him and then taking from him and giving to me. I felt it in every atom of my being. Whatever that multi-colored wind brought with it was inside of us. Both of us. Together.

But it wasn't just in us. It changed us. Somehow. Both of us. I felt the change in my companion even as I felt it in myself because, somehow, we were joined by that wind. For a brief space of time, we were one person.

I pressed harder against the rock and prayed as the wind moved through our bodies separately and together, deeper and still deeper until it reached the core of our beings. It was cold and hot at the same time, and it touched every particle of our beings.

It wanted us. Both of us. I felt the wanting and knew the man against me, protecting me, also felt it. We were both afraid. Terrified. And there was nothing either of us could do except press harder against that rock and wait for it to end and hope we survived.

Then the wind moved on. The body that had been pressed so hard against me went slack as the wind died and the howling lessened and a few, faint beams of sunlight penetrated the space between the rocks. As those welcome beams touched us, the electrically charged fog lightened. Lessened. Then it gradually disappeared and my body once again belonged to me, and I no longer felt like I was joined with the stranger who'd experienced the wind with me.

I followed his gaze and saw the cloud climbing past us, high and then higher still into the sky but faster than it had climbed the valley, and now that it had unlimited space in which to spread it grew thinner and weaker until, in less time than I could believe possible, it dissipated entirely, leaving the sky once again the soft blue of a summer morning.

The gentle summer day was exactly as it had been before the wind came.

We separated and stood for a long time staring at one another until I asked, in a shaky voice, "What just happened?"

"I wish I knew." His voice, too, was unnatural. Of course it was. "All I can say is that we just survived something out of a horror movie."

"Did you feel it? Was it inside us?"

"It was. I felt it too."

What was there to say to something like that? We stood in silence for a very long time as the sun came out stronger and we moved slowly, carefully, experimentally, out from between the rocks and into warm, welcome rays of sunshine. We were silent as we sought to come to grips with the fact that we'd both experienced the same absolutely impossible thing.

"But it's over." He spoke in a reassuring tone of voice that didn't fool me one bit. Did the military train people to pretend nothing was wrong when the world around you was coming apart? It must. "It's over and we're still here. Whatever it was, it's gone, and we're okay, and that's all that matters."

Ignoring the fact that we were somehow changed, and he knew that to be true as surely as I did. I knew because of the way we'd been joined. I'd felt it in him as surely as I'd felt it in me. But I said nothing because what was there to say?

We slowly moved back to the railing we'd left in such a hurry. It was sturdy and had survived the wind, but we had to pick our way through the mass of detritus the multi-colored horror had left.

Leaves, twigs, small and large branches, stones and larger rocks, and a lot of dirt had been sucked into the vortex and dropped as it went past and into the sky.

I pointed to the building at the bottom of the valley. "They do some kind of research down there."

"Do you think they made the wind?"

"No one knows what they do because they don't say, and there are always guards at the entry so no one can find out anything. Hikers are turned away regularly."

I knew because the protesters had told me so when they returned after the building was done and occupied. They'd come to make sure I knew the building represented evil incarnate and that if I'd helped before it was built that evil might not have come to our quiet part of the country.

My military type companion said nothing. He didn't respond to my accusatory tone of voice. But he did stare momentarily at the almost invisible building, as if doing so would answer any questions he might have. Then he looked away.

I spoke again, not because I had anything to add but because I needed to talk to someone, anyone, and he was the only other person in the area. The only person who'd understand what I'd just experienced, and I needed to talk but couldn't bring myself to talk about the wind itself because it shouldn't have existed but did. So I said the only thing I could think to say. "I'm Zoe Smith."

"Tate Brewster." We stared at each other still more because we didn't know what else to do. What to say.

How to come to grips with what had happened. Then Tate Brewster cocked his head and considered me with an odd expression. I couldn't imagine what he was thinking as he looked me up and down, from head to toe, and asked, "Would you do that again?"

I didn't know what he meant, and my puzzled expression showed it. "Would you introduce yourself again?" Seeing my confusion, he added, "I have a hard time remembering stuff. I'm terrible with names."

He lied. People like him always remember things they wish to remember. Of course they do. An excellent, trained memory goes with the ability to see everything and think quickly in an emergency, as he'd just done. I figured it was the military thing. Which meant there was a reason for his wanting me to repeat my name. I just didn't know what the reason was.

But I did as he requested. "My name is Zoe Smith." I gave Tate a questioning look. He correctly interpreted my look as asking why he wanted information he already knew.

He half nodded. "You are right. My request has nothing to do with actually introducing ourselves."

Then he did an odd thing. He introduced himself to me. Again. Just as he'd done less than a minute earlier. "I'm Tate Brewster." When I didn't react, he said, "Please, if you don't mind, let's introduce ourselves a third time. I'll go first. But this time when I say my name, watch my lips."

Tate Brewster repeated his name and as he spoke, I saw what he wanted me to see. What I'd not noticed until he called attention to it. What I couldn't avoid seeing now that I knew what it was. It was that obvious. And that scary.

I now thought my words instead of speaking them out loud so he'd know I'd seen what he wanted me to see. *"We aren't talking out loud. There is no sound. We are communicating with our minds and nothing else."*

He nodded. Without either of us uttering a single word, we'd introduced ourselves to each other. With our minds alone.

As the truth of what was happening dawned on me, fear crept through me. Sheer, unadulterated terror.

Then he spoke. Out loud, intentionally so, because we needed sound. We needed it because spoken words were normal. "How did we do that? Talk without sound?"

I spoke out loud too, also intentionally, thinking each word as I spoke because I suddenly was afraid and needed to know the world still worked in a normal way. That I could speak normally if I chose to do so. That I was normal. I looked straight at him and asked, "What was in that horrible, awful, terrible wind?"

Our next words were said together. By both of us. In tandem. We spoke with our minds, but we also used our voices. We spoke both out loud and mentally. We looked at each other fully and together we asked the question that was on both of our minds. "What did that wind do to us? What have we become?"

CHAPTER 2

"We have to tell someone." A doctor. A psychiatrist. A paranormal researcher. Someone. Anyone.

"No." Tate Brewster's reply was swift and adamant. An order. "That's the one thing we must not do."

"Why not? We need help. We should get it as soon as possible."

One eyebrow rose as he invited me to know what he was thinking. "What will they do when they find out we can talk without speech? That we are telepathic?" Because that's what we were. Telepathic. I tested the word. It had never applied to me. But it did now.

My sudden understanding of his meaning hit hard. He was right not to want to tell anyone. "We'll be examined, that's what will happen. They'll do things to us."

"We'll become lab rats."

"Taken apart and put under a microscope." I looked at the research facility at the bottom of the valley, the place we'd most likely be taken. I shuddered.

Tate's eyes narrowed and he folded his arms and

spread his legs slightly as he thought things through more completely. "On the other hand, maybe it's not as bad as we think. Maybe this thing, this telepathy, will disappear just as rapidly as the wind came and went. Perhaps this really weird ability will disappear, and it'll happen in a few minutes, hours at the most."

The thought was reassuring. "If that should happen after we tell someone, we'll feel foolish because we won't be able to do it anymore."

"But even then, the attention won't end. It won't be the end of our being examined and experimented on."

"Because they'll want to know how it happened even though it'll be gone. They'll try to replicate it. To bring it back."

"They'll do things to us."

"And those things will be done over and over again."

So we agreed to say nothing.

"But let's keep in touch." I squirmed but felt strongly about what I was saying. "I don't know why, but I suspect it could be important."

He didn't laugh. Instead, he nodded. "I agree. We should exchange contact information. Just in case."

I had a small notebook in my pocket with my shopping list for my city excursion. I tore pages out, and we exchanged names and contact information. For Tate there was just a cell phone number. "I'm not settled yet. Just out of the Army and looking for work."

"Not that we'll need to contact one another because surely you are right. This weird ability will be gone soon. Before I reach the city." I looked around at the devastation wrought by the strange weather phenomena. "Probably as soon as we leave this place."

Then I added because I wanted to say something, "I was on a shopping trip. Rain boots."

He smiled a half smile. "Because the forecast is for rain." His reply made me feel better. Rain boots were part of a normal life. I was normal.

We headed for the rest area parking lot and our vehicles. They were still there, untouched, as the wind had blown straight up the valley and then up into space. We each climbed into our vehicles, and I started the engine. Tried to start it. And failed. It was dead.

Tate's old truck started just fine, but he noticed I was having trouble so, instead of leaving, he joined me. "Problem?"

"It won't start."

He frowned and gestured for me to let him try but he couldn't start it either. "Let me check a couple things." He was soon beneath the hood but came up shaking his head that he saw nothing wrong. "Might be the battery. I can jump it."

"It's new."

He tried anyway, but it wasn't the battery. He tried starting my car again but gave up after a few tries. "I don't know what's wrong unless the ignition is shot."

"Is that likely?"

He leaned against the back of the seat and considered the dashboard. "Maybe." He slanted a look towards me. "You could have been sold a lemon. Or more likely, if any part of that wind reached the parking lot, then your electronic ignition is fried."

His collector truck was old enough not to have electronics. "I'll call for roadside assistance."

"If that's the cause, then other electronics might be gone too. Like your phone." I tried my phone, and it was dead. "I'm guessing your car might need to be towed somewhere because if I'm right then all the electronics are fried."

I slumped until he said, "I have a tow rope in my truck." A slight flush spread across his face. "When you drive something this old it's best to be prepared. But that means I can tow you somewhere." His eyebrows rose. "If you want."

"I appreciate any help you can give."

"It's the least I can do. That wind did a number on us, but it also did a number on your car and that means you need a tow." Something close to a grin spread all the way across his face, the first complete expression that wasn't grim for either of us since the wind almost blew us to smithereens. "By the time we get this car to a repair shop, maybe this weird thing that happened will be gone." Then he added, "And we can tear up the contact info and go on our happy ways."

I seconded the motion as he retrieved a tow rope and we hooked our vehicles together and set out for the nearest repair shop. No more shopping trip for me, I could only hope repairs could be done quickly so I could at least be home for what would now be lunch followed by whatever else I'd do for the rest of the day.

The nearest town was tiny, a hamlet, with a sign saying 'Montclair, Unincorporated,' and one repair shop owned by the man who also owned the town's only coffee shop and just about everything else in the one-street semi-town.

Employees ran his various businesses, but if they needed a day off he took over, though if two people got sick it meant one or another of his enterprises had to be shut down until at least one employee could return to work. I'd loved that aspect of small town life when I moved there. Now I wasn't so sure.

I hoped the repair shop would be open. I prayed it would be. And it was, but the necessary parts weren't available and wouldn't be available for a week, possibly several weeks. Seems the hamlet was too small to keep a large inventory, and the supply chain wasn't working well, so no one knew when ordered parts would arrive. I'd simply have to wait. And I had no way to get home or return to town when my car was ready. I was dejected, and it showed.

Tate Brewster, seeing my expression, suggested we adjourn to the coffee shop next door to discuss options. After climbing onto a couple of chairs at the bistro tables at the front, Tate leaned back in what was most likely a signature gesture and waited until our cappuccinos arrived and I'd taken a good swig and settled down a bit. Was patience another of his traits? Perhaps another military thing?

"I can drive you home." He straightened. "I'm in no hurry. As I said earlier, I'm kind of winging life right now. Looking for work but not in too much of a hurry to find it. So a few miles out of my way, and a bit of time out of my non-schedule, isn't a big deal."

"It's not just getting home now, it's also getting back to town when it's fixed." I swirled my cappuccino ruefully. "It's a small town. Things don't always go smoothly."

He frowned. Thought a minute. "Is there a campground nearby? I've been camping some of the time and have the stuff in my truck. I'll gladly stay a while. Until you have transportation again. It'll be a break from looking for work."

I considered his offer. "That's generous of you."

He shrugged. "Not really. Like I said, I'm winging life right now, and this area is gorgeous. I'll enjoy every minute of a stay here." Then he added, "If there's a campground."

I sagged. "There isn't." Lots of resorts and motels for tourists but no campgrounds. Then I brightened. "But I have an idea." He put down his cappuccino to listen. "Please don't take this the wrong way but you can stay with me." I explained. "I have three bedrooms. Two are upstairs and there's a bath there so you'll have privacy and plenty of space." Then I added, "It's just an idea. Don't feel obligated."

His eyes met mine over his cappuccino. "Are you sure? We're strangers."

"Not really. I don't think we are strangers. Not anymore. You saved my life a while back, and you towed my car into town. I suspect that means we're past the stranger thing." Then I remembered something and laughed. "Besides, I keep a Glock beside my bed and my cop father taught me how to use it." No reason for him to know my father gave up on my becoming a good shot and settled for me being mediocre.

He laughed too, spilling cappuccino onto his plaid shirt. "Good to know." He dabbed at the spill with a napkin. "So if anyone tries to break in while I'm there, I'll just roll over and go back to sleep because you'll have the situation well in hand."

I laughed too. "And by the time the car is repaired this thing that's happened to us will be over and done with."

"And we'll have to communicate verbally instead of mentally."

At which moment we realized we were the locus of attention in the small coffee shop because at no time since entering had we said a single word out loud. As we realized what was happening and that we were attracting attention, we started talking out loud and a little too loudly. Soon attention drifted elsewhere and we relaxed, but the incident had been revealing.

"We'll have to be careful." Said out loud.

"I don't want any more attention than necessary." Also spoken audibly.

Tate finished his cappuccino. "How far is your place?"

"Five miles. Why? Does it matter?"

He rose. "Because if it's all the same with you I'd just as soon get out of here before we forget to talk out loud again and someone asks questions, and your place is the logical place to go."

I joined him, and we left the coffee shop, told the repair man to call me when my car was fixed, and headed out of town. Soon Tate pulled into my driveway and stared at my Cape Cod in the depths of the forest. "Nice." He turned one way and another to take in the forest on all sides. "No neighbors. Do you live alone?"

"Yes, but don't forget that Glock and that I know how to use it."

"Trust me, I won't forget, but I'm glad you don't have neighbors so we don't have to pretend we're still normal while I'm here."

I looked at my home from his viewpoint and wondered if there'd be more questions beyond was this my house. Like how did I earn a living so far from anywhere, and why did I live in the middle of nowhere? The questions I'd been asked when my friends and family learned I'd bought a house so far from cities and towns.

I was fortunate, and I knew it. My great-aunt had left me enough money to not have to work if I was careful about finances. I wasn't even close to being rich, but that inheritance paid cash for a house in an area of low cost, and my needs were few.

Plus, my art degree was proving useful. I sold a few things to tourists to supplement my inheritance. It was a good life and, as I looked at my home through Tate's eyes, I once more knew I'd made the right decision to move there. Though as we climbed the porch steps, I cautioned him about the railing that needed fixing and might just come loose if either of us touched it because that person just might end up tumbling head over heels into the yard.

The railing was one of the reasons I could pay cash for the Cape Cod. It was a fixer upper. But I wasn't the fixer upper type. I'd fallen in love with the house and locale and figured I could learn carpentry and fix that and the several other things that needed attention. Some day. It hadn't happened yet, and things were falling apart a little more each day.

We went inside, and I dropped my purse and sweater on the table and wondered what to do next. The day stretched ahead, most of it anyway, and the sun shone so bright it hurt, and it was hard to believe we'd almost been killed a short time ago.

CHAPTER 3

"It'll take a day or so. Maybe more. Probably a lot more." Tate looked around.

"What'll take a day or so?"

He gave me an oblique look that said he hoped his next words wouldn't hurt my feelings. "Securing that loose porch railing and some of the other things I see that could use attention." When I didn't react negatively to him insulting my house, he added, "If you want me to. Because I have the time if you have the tools and some wood somewhere in case anything turns out to be rotten."

I turned squarely towards him. "Please do. The railing is a lawsuit waiting to happen." I told him where to find tools, and that we could head to the nearest somewhat larger town that actually had a lumber yard if he needed wood.

I hadn't wanted to pay a home remodeler to do the job because it would make a sizeable dent in my bank account, but I could afford a little lumber.

It turned out I needed more than a little lumber after he inspected the entire house and found every single thing that needed fixing, but the total was still reasonable. He said he could get at least a few things fixed if I was willing to let him stay a 'bit longer' than until my car was repaired. "I'll be forever grateful, and if you find anything else that's a lawsuit waiting to happen, let me know."

I showed him the upstairs bedrooms. They were practically identical. He chose the one with early morning sun, and that told me he was a morning person. "Make yourself breakfast or whatever you want, but don't wake me up." He agreed, and I thought he was laughing silently as he hauled his belongings up the stairs and stowed them neatly in the dresser in what I assumed was the military way. Then I left him to see about dinner.

As I put together a quick meal, something odd happened. He called. I thought he called. I stepped out of the kitchen and went to the foot of the stairs, but he didn't appear. Then I realized that he didn't need to talk physically because we were now telepathic. So I sort of closed my eyes and directed a question to him.

"Did you call me?" I asked telepathically because I thought perhaps he'd called telepathically to find out whether we could communicate when separated.

"No, but it's interesting that we can do this even when we are so far apart that we couldn't hear each other's normal speech."

"Dinner will be ready in about an hour."

"It'll be an unusual meal. Rather quiet."

"Noble won't like that. He'll think he's being punished."

"Noble?"

"My dog. A black Lab."

"I didn't know you had a dog."

"He's outside. He'll come when he's hungry."

That was the extent of the conversation, but I mulled it over while cooking and letting in Noble when he came to the door, and while setting the table, and also as Tate came downstairs and entered the kitchen.

As I strained noodles for spaghetti, I realized I'd been aware of each and every movement he'd made from the moment he entered my house until dinner, and it wasn't because of any telepathic conversation. But I somehow knew when he went to the bedroom window to look out over the yard and check the depths of the forest.

I knew when he cleaned up in the bathroom. I knew when he drummed his fingers on the dresser. I didn't know why he drummed them, but decided he was considering whether to come down immediately or wait to be called. But I couldn't read his actual thoughts. Not the words he was thinking. So the telepathy only happened if one of us wanted the other to hear what we were saying. That was a relief.

But what was with that other – sensing? Nothing, I decided. I maybe knew what he'd done upstairs but there was no special sensing involved. I knew because they were the normal things for someone in his situation to do, and I merely had an overactive imagination and was just guessing. So I took a deep breath and told myself to return to the normal world, and finish making dinner.

But he was right about dinner being unusual. Noble spent the meal looking from me to Tate and back as if wondering why it was so quiet when there was normally conversation with company. But when I put the scraps in his bowl, he forgot about us and concentrated on food.

"Nice dog. I'll start on the porch railing in the morning."

"He's a foodie, and I'll be so happy to have that railing stay where it belongs."

I wanted to ask what he'd done before dinner. While he was upstairs. Whether my guesses about his activities were right. But I didn't because such questions would be intrusive, not to mention I was afraid to know the answer.

We spent a peaceful evening on the porch watching the sun go down and discussing the loose railing instead of what had happened to us at the rest stop. Because what was there to say? Then we went to bed and pretended everything was normal.

I didn't sleep. I couldn't stop listening for sounds from the upstairs bedroom. I heard none but still couldn't sleep, and I had the oddest feeling that Tate was doing the same thing. I only dropped off when the deepest dark that comes before dawn turned the night inky black and I couldn't make out my hand in front of my face.

I slept late. I suspected Tate did too, but couldn't know for sure because he was a morning person and so would be up before any decent night person would consider opening their eyes even if he'd not slept well. Sure enough, when I left my bedroom, there was evidence of a quick breakfast and the sounds of manual labor on the porch. I started for the door to see how he was doing. Then I stopped.

Because I knew how he was doing. I knew the wood wasn't rotten because I felt his relief that he didn't have to get new boards. I knew there was paint in the shed that matched the paint he'd need because I knew he'd checked the shed to see if there was anything inside that might help. I knew he'd found the left-over paint from when the house had been painted a year or so earlier.

What was this new thing we shared? This sensing, or whatever it was. Something beyond telepathy? And did I really know these things? Or did I just guess at them?

When he entered the kitchen and saw me awake, his cheerful mien said he was pleased and had made the right decision to stick around and be a temporary handyman.

Our looks met. I went on mental alert. Did he know things about me like I knew things about him? Private things?

Our looks veered away quickly, but the brief connection solidified my need to have my life back because I was surely thinking weird thoughts and didn't know if they were about what had happened or about the man who, for reasons beyond normal logic, stood in my kitchen. Or both. And I didn't want him reading my mind.

He spoke. "No breakfast for me. I already ate."

"You're speaking out loud. No telepathy?" Perhaps it was fading.

"It's not gone."

"There's no one around. So why speak out loud?"

"I'm practicing." His lips moved, and I could hear his words. "Yesterday people looked at us oddly because we were talking telepathically. We shouldn't let that happen again. You do whatever you like. You can talk telepathically and I promise to listen. But I'm going to talk normally even when I don't have to."

"You're right. We should act normal in every way, and that includes talking out loud. I'll do the same." Though nothing was normal about our situation.

He'd been checking out my wobbly porch railing and probably some of the other things that needed the attention of a good handyman so I spoke. "You said you were looking for work. What kind of work, exactly? Maybe I know someone." Sneak up to my idea. Pretend I wanted to help him find any kind of work instead of wanting him to stick around until my fixer-upper house was completely fine.

He shrugged. "Whatever. I'm open to suggestions. I figure something will come along. Until then I have what I saved while in the service so I'm okay." He almost smiled. Not quite but it was close. "Don't worry about me. I can stick around until your place is up to par." He knew exactly what I'd been thinking and there hadn't necessarily been weird sensory stuff involved. Just common sense. I hoped.

"You can stay here until you find a job if you want. Your work in exchange for room and board." I sighed because the Cape Cod was old. "There's always something that needs fixing."

"So I noticed, and it's a deal." He reached for my hand. Took it in his.

An electric shock sparked between us.

We both jumped.

"What was that?"

"Static electricity?" But it wasn't that, and we both knew it wasn't. It was different.

Tate's eyes narrowed. He started to touch me again but stopped with his hand inches from mine as he silently asked if he should continue. I nodded that he should, and he touched my hand and the same thing happened again, only differently. No shock this time, just a strange thrumming sensation that started with our clasped hands and spread slowly and inexorably through my body as he held my smaller hand in his larger one and the same thing happened with him.

He didn't let go, and I didn't pull away, as we stared at one another and wondered what was happening. It wasn't painful, but it definitely wasn't normal, and it had to be something to do with the wind. Some weird kind of after effect. There was no other possible explanation.

"What is it?"

"I don't know."

"We'll figure it out." His eyes held mine and forbid me to be afraid as we spoke without words. As he forgot his vow to only speak out loud because what had just happened had blown his mind as it had blown mine.

But somehow, as we stood there bound together by a simple holding of hands, the thrumming lessened and retreated into some part of my body I hadn't know existed and settled into me in a comfortable way similar to when I was a little kid and heard my parents working around the house and knew the world was good. I'd felt safe all those years ago. Holding hands with Tate brought that same sense that things were okay.

Something was happening with Tate too. I saw it in his face. There was uncertainty, followed by surprise at this new thing that was happening, and the same eventual reassurance I'd felt that it was okay. Because I'd given back to him the reassurance he'd given me? Probably not. The man was grounded. Unflappable.

Tough. He didn't need reassurance.

Tate dropped my hand. Rubbed his own. Looked to see if I was doing the same and nodded slightly when he saw I was. "That was weird. Different. Not telepathy. But not bad, either. It was – okay."

"Is this going to continue? Will something new and strange happen to us every day?"

"I don't know. I do know that it didn't feel wrong." The wind had been wrong. The telepathy had been mind-blowing. This new thing wasn't either of those things.

I followed his thoughts. "What just happened now wasn't scary. Or disruptive. But the very fact that it happened is scaring me to death. I don't like it when impossible things happen."

"I'm with you on that." His head tilted and his eyes smiled, though his face didn't. "And it's still morning. There's lots of time for more weird things."

His words were so appropriate and normal that I couldn't help myself. I laughed. I needed a break, and laughter is the best break there is.

I dropped into a chair and put my head down on the table and laughed so hard tears fell, and I didn't know if they were tears of laughter or of fear, but it didn't matter because they somehow got me to a different place. A better place.

Tate, still standing, put a hand on my shoulder and when nothing new and scary happened, when his touch was just a touch and not some weird sensation, he began to laugh with me. I wondered in some corner of my mind if he'd touched me to see if anything further would happen or to comfort me. Or if it was his way of telling me I was truly funny.

I didn't care why he did it. I simply, greedily, took into me all the possible meanings of that simple gesture and was glad for it and, with that acknowledgement, knew that not only was I glad for laughing, I was glad for Tate. And to think we'd almost gone our separate ways, and I'd have had to deal with the result of that wind without him. The thought made me shudder and I put my hand over his, and we stayed that way for a while. Not speaking, not talking out loud or telepathically, just being together.

Then I spent the rest of the day avoiding him because I was afraid I might accidentally touch him and was terrified about what the touching might do. He also avoided me, probably for the same reason. If we didn't know whether a simple touch would be just a touch or something totally weird, avoidance was best.

There were a lot of things for him to do that didn't involve me. The Cape Cod was a disaster. The railing was in pieces, the doors on my kitchen cabinets hung crooked, and there were a dozen or so other things about my much beloved house that needed the care of a fixer upper. There were so many projects that he had to draw up plans and make a list of everything needed to do the job right. It was a long list.

I made pizza for dinner and suggested we head for the tiny nearby hamlet the next day to see how my car repairs were coming and stock up on staples because there'd now be two people living in my house instead of just one.

I pretended that was why we were going. Because we needed more food. Actually, both the freezer and pantry were overflowing, but that night as I lay in bed awaiting sleep, I got honest with myself and admitted the real reason for the trip was to see normal people and prove to myself that I was still human enough that I could function in normal, human society. That I wasn't a freak, and by extension, Tate wasn't either.

But I dreaded the coming morning when, at some point, whether intentional or accidental, we'd touch. When that happened, when my body once again came into contact with Tate's, especially after so many hours apart, what would be the result?

Nothing? Something? I didn't know. The not knowing scared me.

CHAPTER 4

I was up early the next morning, which was unusual for me, and I hadn't slept well so, in addition to my usual morning sluggishness, I was tired. I reminded myself a dozen times not to be cranky around my guest.

Then Tate came bouncing downstairs wide awake and all smiles, and the tiredness fell away, and I wanted to touch him and steal some of that early morning energy for myself. I didn't, of course, because I was afraid something awful would happen if I did. If we touched. But I gathered as much of that energy as possible from a safe distance.

He asked a logical question. "Do we have a shopping list? Food? Maybe other staples?"

I agreed that we should have a list, so we dropped into chairs across from one another at the kitchen table and made one. We carefully didn't touch. Instead, we shoved the list back and forth across the table.

The listed items pretty much duplicated what I already had in the house, but I didn't tell Tate that because with each passing moment and the near-misses of almost touching him as we passed the growing list back and forth, I felt an increasing need to be in the normal, every-day world, the world without telepathy, so I needed in the worst way imaginable to go to town whether the pantry needed stocking or not.

But the strange thrumming of the day before started anyway, even though we didn't touch. Then it grew. Then it grew still stronger. I didn't know if Tate felt it too until he looked at the list one last time and then slowly and very carefully shoved it to one side.

He pointed to the scrap of paper on the table. "Is it the list that's doing it?" His look lifted to mine. "Is the list causing whatever is happening to us now?" He avoided the scrap of paper like it was poison. "Is it because we're touching the same piece of paper even though we're not touching it at the same time?"

"You feel it too?"

"Of course." He nodded. "If this keeps up, soon we won't be able to be in the same house without it happening. It'll be that bad."

I bit my lip. I didn't want him to be right. Whatever was happening to me – to us – was so strange that I wanted someone near me who was going through the same thing. Someone I could talk to, and that person was Tate. So I wanted him around, and I didn't want to have to avoid him.

He took a few gulps of air and seemed to come to a conclusion. He reached across the table for my hands. One upturned eyebrow asked a silent question. Should we touch? I nodded assent but my mouth went dry.

His hand touched mine, and we waited to see what would happen.

The thrumming returned. But it wasn't unpleasant. Perhaps it was even better than it had been yesterday. As our hands slowly, cautiously, clasped tighter and then tighter still, I knew it was okay. The thrumming was warm and comfortable. Not only was it a good feeling, it felt as if I'd been waiting all my life to feel like I felt at that moment.

I sighed in relief and felt Tate's hand grasp mine more fully. Did it affect him too? If so, how did he feel right now? Good? Bad?

He dropped my hand and there was relief in his voice, but his next words didn't tell me much. "It's a strange and very, very odd sensation, but I can live with it." He took both of my hands in his once more, and we sat there for almost ten minutes enjoying the fact that we could touch one another without unnerving consequences.

"We're still normal. Sort of. Still human."

"Except for the fact that we are changed and are still changing." His look nailed me to my seat, daring me to argue. I couldn't.

"We're even more different than we were yesterday. More than immediately after it happened."

His reply was rueful. "I was afraid we'd need something between us in the truck to keep us from touching each other. And that we'd have to use two shopping carts instead of one because we'd not dare both touch the same one at the same time." We stared at each other because neither of us knew what to say.

Then something unexpected happened. Something nice. His lips turned up in a smile that made the morning a thousand times better than the evening before and the long, dark night had been. I breathed a sigh of relief that life was still good. But time was passing, so I rose and made a proposition I'd been considering since yesterday. "Let's have breakfast in town. My treat."

I suspected he knew I wanted to be in a normal

cafe eating a normal breakfast surrounded by normal people. The normalcy would be like a security blanket. I didn't want to say anything out loud because I doubted a former military type would understand such an infantile need. But his quiet smile said he knew.

In the truck, just before reaching town, while idly watching the forest through the window, I broke what had been total silence up to that point and spoke, hoping not to make a complete fool of myself. "Can you stick around until this thing goes away? Even if the repairs are completed before then and the house is functional? I want someone I can talk to who knows what I'm going through."

He reacted so fast he almost drove off the road. After managing to bring the truck back into the right lane, he said, "What you just said – how you said it – the exact words – is odd because I was thinking the same thing. Precisely the same thing. Same words, even." He slowed as he turned carefully onto the main street.

I gulped. "That's perfectly normal considering the circumstances."

"Of course." He kind of shook his shoulders the way people do while recovering from a shock. "You're right. It's a coincidence. Same thoughts led to the same words. No big deal." But we both stared straight ahead instead of at each other.

At the repair shop, the mechanic had good news. "It won't be as long as I thought. The parts are available and are being shipped as I speak. So soon your car will be good to go. A few days, maybe one week instead of several."

On that good news we headed for the only café in

town. We found a booth and looked around. I recognized an elderly couple from previous encounters in town and we nodded. The place was exactly what I needed, and I relaxed.

The waitress gave us menus. Tate took his, but then shoved it aside without opening it. "I'll have the special." He tipped his head towards me. "So will Zoe, but sunny side up for her."

She wrote down our orders and left as I tried to push down the nausea that suddenly threatened to turn my stomach inside out. "How'd you know without looking, what the special consists of? And how'd you know how I want my eggs?"

Tate frowned. "Two eggs, bacon, and toast." His frown deepened. "Isn't it?" and I nodded.

He realized what I was getting at, and his eyes went wide. "How'd I know that? I've never been here before. Never seen the menu." He moved his body, looking to one side and then the other, as if the booth was suddenly too small, too confining. "And why do I know you like your eggs sunny side up?"

We stared at each other. "You know those things because that's the special at most cafes in the entire country. And most people prefer their eggs sunny side up."

I fiddled with my napkin. I wrapped and unwrapped the silverware three times and thought about what was happening. Had been happening. Was still happening. "I wish whatever has taken over would go away. I wish I didn't see everything that happens as something different and scary when it's probably just normal, everyday life."

His lips pressed together. "Don't worry about it.

Even if what just happened was part of what's going on with us, even if we are permanently weird, this thing won't beat us. I promise you that."

I took the careful controlled breath I'd learned in some obscure meditation class. "We have a new power. We can do something we couldn't before yesterday. We can talk without sound. And maybe there's more. Maybe. But compared to the amazing things some people can do, it's no big deal." I didn't fool him one bit. He knew exactly how big of a deal it was. We were telepathic and perhaps more.

After a silent, somber breakfast, we wondered through town, all one street of it. As we reached the end, the predicted rainstorm burst overhead. The storm that had sent me shopping for rain boots.

The forecaster had been right. It was a torrential downpour. Rain fell from the sky so hard and thick it made a curtain across the street. I could barely make out the stores on the other side. Water poured across the sidewalk, over the curbs, and along the gutters.

We ran for the safety of the nearest store. It catered to tourists and had everything they'd left at home that they later discovered to their dismay they needed. Like rain ponchos. We bought two.

I also purchased rain boots even though they cost way more than in any big box store in the city, and Tate got himself a pair. "If I'm going to be around for a while, I might need them." He slanted a look at me. "Because, to answer your question of earlier, I'm here to see this thing through to the end, whenever that is."

He wandered off to check out the sale isle, and I headed for the front door to see if the downpour had let up enough for us to venture outside. As I passed the clerk, she recognized me. Not my name but that I was local. "Heard the big news?" I said I hadn't. "About that research place?"

I recognized her. She was part of the group that had tried to stop it from being built. "Something nasty happened at the overlook the other day." I pretended surprise and waited for more information. "Word on the street is that research station created a wind." She shook her head. "Can you imagine it? They made the wind blow. As if it doesn't blow enough already."

"Really?" I forced myself to look casual.

"According to my sources – and they are usually right – the wind blew up the canyon super strong because it's so narrow that it confined it and turned it into a real blast. My guy said there was debris all over the overlook. It had to be closed for hours while a cleanup crew hauled all that stuff away. That's how he knew. He was part of the cleanup crew, and they aren't done yet."

"No, I hadn't heard." I managed to make my voice normal, but it was an effort.

She knew I hadn't opposed the research facility when it was built, and she wanted me to know what my lack of concern had done. The catastrophe that had happened because of the disinterest of people like me. Her frown said that was why she'd passed on the information. That and her upturned nose.

I pasted a smile on my face and said the rain had let up, and wasn't that nice? She grunted her disbelief that anyone could be so callus about the way humanity was treating the earth and retreated behind the counter that she sprayed with disinfectant. I didn't mention that the disinfectant was probably contaminating the entire store. Instead, I went to find Tate and tell him the downpour had become a steady rain that our ponchos could handle.

"Is this a good deal?" He held up a hunting knife. "I could use a knife like this, and it's a good brand, but I don't know what prices are like around here."

"What do you think about what just happened? What the clerk said?" When he didn't react, I added telepathically, *"Do you know what just happened? What the clerk just said? I'm pretty upset."*

His forehead wrinkled with effort, but he shook his head. *"What's wrong?"* He furtively checked out the clerk who was still giving me the evil eye. *"Whatever she said, ignore it. She seems to be the slightly unhinged type."*

I giggled because he'd said the right thing and lifted my spirits. I repeated my conversation with the clerk. He put the knife down. *"That's more than interesting. What say we get out of here and go someplace where we can talk without her staring daggers our way?"*

At the door, we paused to don our new ponchos. Then we stepped into rain that had lessened and was now a summer rainstorm. We headed for his truck, pausing to pick up cappuccinos in nonrecyclable Styrofoam cups the clerk would have hated.

I looked out the window, my thoughts in a whirl. About the telepathy, of course. And maybe a new thing, maybe a sense of knowing that went beyond guessing. I didn't know about that extra thing, but as I stared at the town, I acknowledged that for some reason I couldn't define I wondered if it was because of weird things happening, or if he was simply a hunk and my body was responding accordingly.

I hoped he didn't know what I was thinking. I turned away a bit more so he couldn't read my face. I hoped he couldn't read my mind, but didn't know for sure.

When had I first felt something for him? And why? And what would the future hold?

I sighed because my life was so messed up I couldn't possibly know where normal emotions ended and my strange new ones began. I shivered and Tate noticed. "Is something wrong? Are you cold? Are you wet? We don't need to talk now. I'll get you home where you can dry out." So he hadn't read my mind. He didn't know what I was thinking. I sighed in relief.

He reached to start the engine but I used my hand to stop him. "I'm dry. It's nothing." That didn't satisfy him, so I searched for an explanation that could be partially true. "It's this crazy weird situation. Just now it hit me all over again. Our lives have changed, and my body reacted."

That part was true. My body was reacting to the man beside me and now I couldn't stop noticing him, and that was in addition to the telepathy, which was intimate in itself. In short, I was a total disaster.

He relaxed. "If you're sure you're okay."

But, as I covertly examined him, I wasn't sure he'd told me everything. Possibly he'd read my mind and knew exactly how I was feeling at that moment. I turned to the window to hide my face that was turning redder and redder as the rain fell in curtains beyond the truck.

CHAPTER 5

I stared out the truck window. Then I opened it, stuck my hand out, and watched it get wet, but not too wet and not too fast. The rain was letting up. As we sat, it had turned into a gentle, all-day rain. I made myself speak normally, meaning out loud. No telepathy involved. "We aren't done shopping. There are still items on our list."

"Stuff for the house repairs."

We finished our cappuccinos and proceeded with the other reason for coming to town. My fixer-upper Cape Cod. We covered ourselves with our new ponchos, and headed for the next store on our list. Hardware. Knobs and hinges and more.

We didn't make it that far. As we passed a narrow opening between buildings, we heard a sound. We hesitated. Looked at one another. Tried to sense what was causing the sound but neither of us recognized it, and it could be someone in trouble, so we turned into the opening to see what was going on.

It was the wrong move. Before our eyes adjusted to the shadows, three punks, each with a weapon – a tire iron, a club, and a chain – surrounded us.

"Your money, or else."

I panicked and forgot how to breathe. Tate, on the

other hand, went into military mode. I knew he was considering which kind of response of the several he undoubtedly knew how to implement was the right one to use in this situation.

He took one look at me and knew I was on the verge of panic. *"Hang on, Zoe. Calm down. This isn't as bad as it seems."*

"They'll hurt us."

"No they won't. They are just teenaged punks. I'll deal with them."

He spread his legs and folded his arms in front of his body. Then he spoke. "If you leave now, we'll pretend this unfortunate incident never happened, and I strongly urge you to do exactly that, and to do it quickly. Before I lose my patience."

The punks stopped their advance. Each checked what the others were doing. They didn't know how to react to Tate's calm, unblinking demeanor. Then they recovered some of their original bluster and started towards us again, but slower, looking to each other for support, afraid of what might happen if Tate's threat wasn't empty.

As they approached, Tate didn't move and didn't blink. He merely tipped his head as if considering his options and he said, *"Give it time. I think it'll work. They are shook up."*

"You're bluffing?"

"Totally, but they don't know that."

Then a thin, middle-aged man with one hand in his coat pocket appeared from behind a dumpster. Strode past the three punks and towards Tate. Slowly, casually, but with intent. "You might fool these three idiots, but you don't fool me."

The hand in his pocket moved. It bulged. "I'm older than they are, and wiser, and the gun in my pocket with my finger on the trigger says you'd be smart to hand over whatever valuables you two have, or it might go off." He paused for effect. "It has a silencer, so no one will hear and come to your rescue." He came a step closer, then stopped mere feet from Tate. "Ten seconds. That's how long you have to decide whether you want to live or die."

Tate didn't move. He continued to stare the man down every bit as insolently as the man stared at him. But he spoke to me telepathically. *"When I tell you to run, run! Don't wait for me and don't stop. Head for the street and keep going until you reach the nearest door, and then go inside and slam the door behind you."*

"What about you?"

"I'll be fine. Just do as I say." Then he added, *"Please."*

A thrumming had begun when the punks first surrounded us. It strengthened as Tate spoke to my mind. It was telepathy, but it was more than that. It said I could trust Tate. He knew what he was doing. He was both competent and experienced. He'd been in situations like this before. I hadn't.

I watched him. His stance. The stillness of his body. I suspected he'd pushed everything from his conscious mind in order to concentrate on what he was going to do next, and that he needed me to do as he said because he couldn't take care of business and take care of me, too.

"Give me some warning so I'll be ready."

"On my count of three. One – two – THREE!"

I ran, but as I reached the sidewalk, in spite of his orders I slowed enough to look back. During the mini second it took me to get that far, Tate had reached for the leader of the group and was taking him down. The element of surprise was on Tate's side, but they were struggling. The three punks were running away as fast as they could move.

I turned back to the sidewalk and ducked into the nearest doorway, where I shook the rain off my poncho and looked around. It was the hardware store we'd been heading for, but it felt like a different world. How could life be normal inside when a robbery was in progress mere yards away?

Was Tate okay? Could he take down the leader of the punks? Should I have stayed in spite of his orders so I could help? I leaned against the wall and prayed that I'd made the right move. I strained to hear something. Anything.

"I'm fine." The words came loud and clear, though no one except me could hear. *"But our dishonest friend won't be walking upright for quite some time."* I slumped in relief, and waited for Tate to join me, which he did in mere moments, strolling casually through the door as if he didn't have a care in the world while I was still barely functional.

"He could have shot you."

"He didn't have a gun."

"How'd you know?" Had he some kind of professional knowledge? Or had he taken a chance?

"Remember the silencer he claimed to have? The pocket on his coat was small. It could hardly hold a pistol let alone his entire hand and a pistol with a silencer attached." After a pause, he added, *"Most*

silencers are rather large." He knew about silencers. Of course he did, and most likely about a lot of other things I couldn't imagine.

I relaxed, and something pooled in me. I felt so warm and safe that I had to remind myself not to let him know how his actions had affected me. I had the strangest wish to throw myself at his body and sob for a long time, but I restrained myself as our looks connected, and he took my arm, and we headed for the aisle with hinges and knobs and anything else he might need to get my fixer-upper house in shape.

Tate told me more of what had happened in the alley as we passed an aisle filled with nails and screws in their small, neat boxes on our way to the hardware we needed for the Cape Cod. *"Back there, things happened fast, but that's okay because I'm used to it. Most important, though, I suspected he was bluffing because his type usually are. I was pretty sure he didn't have a gun. Sure enough to chance it."* He shrugged. *"It was easy."*

"Easy for you. I was afraid the next time I saw you, you'd be lying in a pool of blood."

The incident had turned out okay, but it could have been otherwise. The thought of other potential outcomes got to me. Of blood. Of a body sprawled in that alley. I started to shake. After a few seconds Tate wrapped an arm around me, supporting me, and kept it there while we picked out new hardware for my falling apart kitchen cabinets.

We garnered a few looks in the process. We got smiles from an older woman who probably read romances in her spare time, and received eye rolls from a couple of small boys. We paid for our purchases, and then returned to the truck through what was now a misty rain with a hint of sun shining through that turned the miniature droplets into pure gold.

By the time we reached my house the rain had ended entirely and we didn't need our ponchos. We hauled in our supplies, and put everything away except the hardware that stayed on the kitchen table because it would be used soon.

As Tate helped fill the pantry shelves with our recent acquisitions, placing new items next to ones already there that were identical, he turned away so I wouldn't see his grin. He clearly knew why I'd wanted to go shopping, and that the trip had less to do with needing groceries or hardware and more with getting out into the normal world.

I was embarrassed as I placed a new package of pasta beside a similar old one, accepting that he knew I'd been scared out of my wits while he'd been calm and collected. I knew he didn't know quite what to say. After all, we were in uncharted waters where relationships were concerned.

He finally settled on acknowledging that our situation at the Cape Cod was abnormal. It was something to say, a way of admitting that things were odd between us. "If what's going on bothers you, I can leave."

He looked away for a moment, unsure if this was the right thing to say or whether something else would be more appropriate but he was determined to say something. To fill the growing silence between us as we stocked the pantry. "Maybe it'll be better that way. Perhaps if we are far enough apart, it'll all go away, and there won't be any more telepathy."

"Don't go."

He finished stocking the pantry before turning to me. "What you're feeling right now, I know about it. It's the aftereffect of the robbery, plus how you felt before it happened. The wind. The telepathy. It all came together and hit you hard, and there's no shame in it."

He came close, then, and pulled me to him without asking. I gave up pretending to be tough and in control and went willingly. Some part of me was shocked at my behavior. But it felt so right to relax against his chest that I didn't care.

He patted me awkwardly, and as soon as I recovered, let go of me. I was pretty sure he knew the precise moment I was okay. He felt it in my body against his. We were inches from each other after I was released, so it was easy to look up at him when he said, "I've been thinking. We've not been apart since it happened. I should take the truck and drive somewhere. A few miles, maybe a lot of miles. I want to see if we can still talk to each other telepathically when we are separated by a sizable distance."

It was a good idea. Why hadn't we thought of it before? "You do that. We should know." Then I added, "But don't forget to come back."

"Don't worry about that. I'll come back. You don't have your car yet, and there's still a lot of work to be done around here."

We adjourned to the porch then, where we watched the sun turn the last raindrops into pure gold as they fell from the porch roof onto the recently refurbished railing. I leaned happily on the railing and got wet and didn't care because all that mattered was that it held my weight. Tate joined me, and soon we were both sopping wet. It felt good and right.

He turned towards me, but didn't touch me. Instead he considered me with my arms in wet shirtsleeves and, out of nowhere, said, "We should talk about stuff. About us."

"Us?"

"I think you know what I mean."

We faced each other in that golden mist, and Tate's eyes glinted. "We should decide what we want to do about these feelings we have for each other that we're trying hard to ignore, and don't pretend you don't know what I'm talking about because I'm pretty sure you do. I'm pretty sure you are experiencing the same feelings that I'm having, only in reverse."

He knew. Of course he knew. Unlike me, though, he wasn't embarrassed about it and wanted to talk.

I listened as he continued. "I never expected to feel this way about anyone, especially someone I just met. But I do, and I'm absolutely positive that you do too. So let's stop pretending it doesn't exist."

"We just met. It's too soon."

He nodded agreement. "Because it might be the telepathy thing and will go away when the telepathy ends."

"Something like that. Do you think that when you are far away it'll fade?"

"Let's find out."

He moved. Pulled his truck keys from his pocket. "It'll only take a few minutes to drive a lot of miles. Then we'll know."

I watched his pickup turn onto the road and waited for something to happen. For normal to return. For the telepathy to go away. But it didn't.

He was gone a long time. A couple of hours. When he returned, he said he'd gone over fifty miles. Far enough that if something was to change, it would have done so. While he was gone the sun had dropped to the horizon and no longer turned the world gold. Instead, dusk was creeping across the yard as he walked back towards me.

He spoke first, standing on the top step. "Distance doesn't make any difference. I now believe that if I went half-way around the world even that wouldn't change anything. I heard every word you said, and you were on the porch and I was fifty miles away."

"Same with me." We'd talked the whole time he was gone. About the rain, and the weather, the repairs still needing to be done, our new ponchos now hanging to dry on the porch, and our new boots beside the door. "I heard your every word loud and clear."

"So now that we know distance doesn't matter, what do we do about it? About us?"

"I don't know." It was the only truthful answer I could give.

We stared into the growing dark until Tate finally said, "Maybe the best thing is to do nothing. To give it time."

"Because maybe it'll fade?"

His laugh showed what he thought about that possibility. I didn't need to be able to read his mind. That laugh said it all.

But it was good advice and I decided to follow it. I'd ignore what was between us in the hope that someday it would be gone. I'd forget what he'd said about his feelings for me because they were probably due to the weirdness of our shared experience. And my feelings for him were most likely due to the same thing.

But I couldn't pretend to feel nothing. That I felt no sparks. As the sun dropped behind the trees my awareness of him was so acute that just being near him was almost more than I could handle, and when I casually went to the farthest part of the porch, I learned that being physically apart didn't make it any easier.

The only improvement was that the night and the mist rising from the recent rain turned him into a shadow. But I still knew he was there. I felt him.

Somehow, though, as darkness descended around us like a cloak, I decided I could manage. I'd avoid him as much as possible. I wouldn't let things escalate because if one day we were once again just a couple of strangers and all the feelings disappeared, well if that happened then I'd be glad I'd not let my feelings overwhelm me.

Because if I let myself obsess over him in the belief that he felt the same, and the feelings on my part didn't end and he simply walked out of my life when normalcy returned, well if that happened I didn't want to spend eternity crying into Noble's soft, sympathetic fur. Noble was a nice dog and deserved better than that.

CHAPTER 6

The next morning, we talked about what to do with the day ahead. I felt odd after the previous night's conversation, and Tate, too, seemed off kilter. He paced back and forth and only stopped when he realized I was watching. "Yesterday it felt wrong to be able to talk telepathically, and today it feels almost normal. Is that a sign of progress?" I didn't answer and he resumed pacing.

He eventually pretended to hunt for hinges for the kitchen cabinets. He avoided looking at me. Then he gave a huge sigh, gave up, and said ruefully, "At the moment, the only thing that's important is that I get these cabinet doors on straight, and add some new, awesome hardware."

As the hours passed and the kitchen slowly became a truly functional space, I decided that normalcy would likely return given enough time. Except wanting normalcy didn't halt my emotional tailspin, and I didn't know if I was in an emotional vortex because of telepathy or because of the man in my kitchen. Or both. And were they inextricably intertwined? I hadn't a clue.

I decided my thought process would drive me insane if I didn't do something, so I headed for the enclosed back porch that I'd turned into an art studio of sorts. I gathered some stuff I'd collected during the many walks I took with Noble that I turned into art and sold for a little extra income. I didn't consider it actual art, but tourists liked it.

Most of the stuff ended up in the trash because I couldn't figure out what to do with it, but some made it onto collages, and I made them on the porch, so the porch was a place of comfort. Noble had always been my long-suffering art critic. His 'woofs' were greatly valued though I was pretty sure the smells on all that stuff reminded him of our walks, and that fact had more to do with his comments than his thoughts on art.

The sound of work elsewhere in the house ended. I listened for what Tate was going to do next. Which project of the list we'd made he'd turn to now. He surprised me. He came through the door, took in my studio, blinked, and tried to come up with an appropriate comment. I saved him the trouble. "Don't even try. I'm not a famous artist, not even close. It's income, not art."

He looked around in awe before removing a handful of colored pebbles from a chair so he could take a seat. "I've been thinking." I waited. He had something on his mind important enough to necessitate a break from the carpentry I'd already realized was something he loved as much as I loved puttering with found objects. "It's about the telepathy. I propose that we go on the offensive."

A military term that was appropriate in the circumstances. "What are you suggesting?"

"That we do some research. We know what happened to us, and we know how it happened, but we don't really know anything about telepathy itself." He waved at the porch, the surrounding forest, and at the miles of wilderness that separated my home from practically everywhere. "We're not going to find out anything just sitting here, and we should know what this is doing to us and is going to do in the future."

"The research facility created a big wind that almost blew us to bits. We know that much. They should be held responsible."

"I agree with you, but I prefer not going there and telling them what they did."

"What else can we do?"

He leaned close. "Why are we sitting around waiting to see what happens next? At the very least, we should find out everything we can about telepathy, so we won't be blind-sided if something new comes along."

I put down the pinecones I'd been hot gluing to a board. "Just how do we do that?"

"I don't know exactly. That's why I'm here instead of fixing your crooked kitchen cabinets. To see if you have any ideas. If you don't, then where's the best place that's reasonably close where we can do some research? And how do we do that research?"

"A library?"

"It would have to be a big one. I suspect the books we'll need are rare enough that anything smaller than a major city library won't have anything."

"Then it'll be a two-hour drive to the city." It was where I did my major shopping and had planned to buy rain boots. "But the library definitely is big. It's huge, and they have rooms with large tables that you can reserve where you can spread books out as much as you like. You can spend the entire day there. Or week if you reserve it for that long." Something I'd learned shortly after moving to my tiny Cape Cod and realizing I needed something to bring in a little money. Their collection of books on art was awesome. "But I don't know what they have regarding telepathy."

"Anything close to telepathy would help. Extrasensory perception. Precognition. Anything."

I checked the time. "It's too late to go there today, but there's still time to call and reserve a room. Maybe we can get one tomorrow."

Noble interrupted our discussion. He woofed. He didn't like being ignored, and when he woofed in that special way it meant I might as well give him what he wanted because he wasn't going to stop woofing until he got it. "After I make the call, want to take a walk with us and see what we can find that might make a collage?"

"Us? Who else do you walk with?"

I patted my dog. "Noble. We take a lot of walks. He hunts squirrels and I hunt for stuff like what you see around you."

He looked perplexed but he said, "Okay. Just don't expect me to find anything. I don't know the difference between a piece of trash and a work of art."

"Most people don't care, and that's good for my business because I don't sell art. I sell memories."

He picked up a couple of pebbles and juggled them. "Nature stuff from a vacation in the woods."

It turned out to be a slow time in the library business so we were able to book a room for the next day. Then we set off for our walk. I slung a tote over my shoulder to hold whatever we found, if anything, and filled a pocket with treats to bribe Noble if he decided to wander and didn't want to come when I called.

"How much property do you own?" Tate asked after half an hour of walking.

"We passed my property line long ago, but I have permission to walk here." I pointed. "See the cleared area ahead? It's a rather nice road the owner had made to get around his property. He's elderly and had a stroke, so he now uses a four wheeler the size of a small car. The road goes near my house, but I like walking through the woods so I didn't head for it right away. Sometimes I find my best treasures under the trees."

We reached the road, and Tate gazed down both directions. Then we set off, and I gathered some dead weeds that would make a nice backdrop for something colorful. I stuffed them in my tote, then we stopped for a while so Noble could investigate a hollow log he was sure was hiding something.

Tate examined the surprisingly smooth but narrow road. I explained. "He had it made right, and it's maintained and is easy for someone who had a stroke to navigate."

"You can't see it until you stumble on it, but a small car would fit with no problem."

"Which was how the owner wanted it."

When Noble finished his futile search for villains in the hollow log, we returned to the Cape Cod and finished out the day with small chores because it was too late to start any major projects.

We somehow ended up on the front porch again, as most evenings, but this time we thought about what to look up when we headed for the city and the library. "Telepathy is the big one."

"If it's at all common, there should be plenty of information. Who has it, and how people get it."

"The one thing I don't want to find out is that we are unique."

I called Noble, who was charging back and forth across the yard chasing imaginary squirrels. He had a thing about squirrels. "What say we walk some more? Noble evidently didn't get enough exercise. I'll show you where my neighbor's road comes close to my house. He visits occasionally." I checked the sky that was already losing daylight. "We'll be back before it's really dark."

Noble was dancing with eagerness to be off because he sensed a walk, one of his favorite things in the whole world. So I led the way through an unusually thick area of brush behind the house that was actually bushes concealing a narrow but easily traversed path that led to the forest road.

Tate examined the path in surprise. "It's almost at your back door but I'd never have guessed it was here." We followed the path until we stepped onto the road that was wide enough for a car but looked like no more than a slight open space between the trees until you were on it. "Easy walking, and Noble likes it."

We followed Noble as he ran up and down the road and in and out of the forest until the rapidly dimming light said it was time to return if we didn't want to end up stumbling around in the dark.

Before Tate headed upstairs to bed, he said, "I can't wait to reach that library and get some answers."

I silently agreed. I could only hope the library had answers and would tell us that Tate and I weren't unique.

CHAPTER 7

The next morning early, after making sure Noble had food and water available and his doggie door was operational, we headed for the city. The sun was up because it rose early in the summer, but it was the deep red of early morning. I settled in the passenger seat, and enjoyed not being the driver, a luxury I'd not experienced since moving to the Cape Cod.

We grabbed breakfast at a drive-through and ate as we went in order to not waste any time, so we reached the library as the doors were being unlocked. We tossed our empty containers in a trash can, and I showed the librarian my card. She pointed to a map of the library, and told us which room was ours and how to find the books we wanted.

"You like the super-natural." Her voice was neutral.

"It's interesting." Her eyebrows went up, and I expected her to say something about classical literature versus scary stuff, but she didn't.

Tate was impressed with the huge ancient building that had started life as a mogul's stone mansion. He looked around. "This place is big enough to need that map she was so proud of."

"Which means if it doesn't have what we're

looking for then we most likely won't find it anywhere."

On that sobering thought, we headed for the stacks and grabbed as many books as we could carry that dealt with telepathy and other supernatural subjects. They had a lot, and we had to make several trips, but that was the deal with that library. If you were in a reserved room doing research of any kind, they didn't limit the number of books you could have. So surely at least one of them would tell us what was happening to us.

It seemed to take forever to collect all the books the library had on those subjects. Every. Single. Book. Then it took even longer to organize them into piles on the huge table that dominated the room. They made several piles. Books on general supernatural phenomena on one side of the table, ones specifically on telepathy on the other. A small desk with a computer was in a corner, but we doubted we'd use it because we had enough books to keep us busy for a week, and we only had the room for one day.

We started through the books, dividing them into those with real information and those written by people who didn't know anything but wanted to get rich pretending to know something. That took a lot of time but made the piles smaller, with the discarded ones piled on top of each other on the tiny desk. Then we started reading.

We came up for air around noon to go find lunch. Upon returning, the sort of friendly librarian waved as we passed her desk. "You two picked a popular topic." We stopped. Backed up enough to ask what she meant. "Telepathy and supernatural phenomena. Lots of interest in those things today. Unusual for this library.

Mostly farmers and such come here, not people wanting to learn about witches and ghosts."

She paused. "But the people today weren't farmers. They were well-dressed and rather unfriendly." She shook her head. "Never met such off-putting people. Reminded me of the men in black everyone talks about."

"Someone besides us is researching this stuff?"

She removed long, leopard print encased legs from the chair they'd been resting on while buffing her nails. "There were several of them, and they all acted like they owned the world, and they all asked the same questions in the same way, and they were all looking for the same information you guys were after." She waved her nails in the air, admiring them and inviting us to do the same. "Wouldn't you think one person asking questions would be enough? But, no, they all had to talk at once."

She dropped her hands to the desk. "But you guys got here first, and did your due diligence at the card files. I doubt there's another book in this building on those subjects beyond what you already have." She stood up, nails forgotten, and leopard print yoga pants hidden behind the tall desk. "And don't worry. They won't bother you. The rooms are private. Off limits to anyone except the people who reserved them."

Tate asked in what I hoped was an offhand way, "Did they ask about us? Since we took all the books?"

She shook her head. "No, but if they had I'd not have told them anything. Not the room or your names. Nothing. And they won't learn anything if they return. Not that they'll return because they were pretty pissed when they discovered the books they wanted weren't available." She fluffed orange hair. "I figure they belonged to some group or other. You know, the kind that chases flying saucers and goes on expeditions looking for Bigfoot."

"Did they say what group they belong to?"

"They didn't and I didn't ask, but I suspect they came from fairly far away because they were thoroughly disgusted at the amount of time they wasted coming all this way. Those were their exact words. 'All this way.' As if they'd spent hours traveling." She settled back into her chair and her job as guardian of the library. "And that's all I know, but be assured you won't be bothered by anyone, not while I'm around."

When we reached our room, I said what we were both thinking. "Does someone know what happened and is doing research the same as we are?"

Tate was grim. "I hope not."

"Who'd know about the wind? We were the only ones affected."

"The people who made it happen would know."

"The research facility at the bottom of the valley."

"Don't jump to conclusions. The people here today might not have had anything to do with a wind that happened days ago. They could have been anyone doing research for any reason at all. A group of paranormal groupies, like the librarian thought. A family wanting to connect with a long-gone ancestor to settle a property dispute. Anyone at all."

"It still bothers me."

"There's nothing we can do about it. She didn't give their names. They probably never said who they were, and that librarian wouldn't tell us if they did. She'd stab us with a nail file just for asking."

We settled in for an afternoon of concentrated research. Tate took telepathy, and I learned about the supernatural. We read for hours and were glad the library stayed open until late in the evening because we'd had no idea how much we'd need to learn when I reserved the room for just one day. We made notes that were irrelevant because every new thing we learned was seared into our consciousness. We were learning about ourselves one book at a time. Except, in a way, we weren't learning about ourselves at all.

"This isn't us." Tate closed the latest book and stretched stiff shoulder muscles.

"What isn't?" I looked up from whatever I'd been reading.

"What I'm reading. According to all the books, we aren't telepathic as it's usually described."

"Why not?"

"We talk to each other mentally exactly as if we were talking out loud. In words. The only difference is that there's no sound involved. Other than that, it's the same as regular speech." He pointed to his current book. "According to this and every other book, telepathy isn't that clearly defined. It's knowing what another person is thinking without necessarily hearing actual words like we do."

"Then it's less than what we have."

"A lot less." He walked restlessly around the room. Pacing. "Or more because I don't know what you are saying mentally unless you choose to say it. Telepaths know things, but they don't always actually hear words not even mentally. Somehow, they just know."

"So what do we have if it's not telepathy?" I riffled the pages of my book on the supernatural. "What we have is supernatural, I know that, because the supernatural includes all kinds of things, and few of them are well defined. It's all kind of vague and is similar to what we have but it can be other things too."

"Which means we are different from other supernatural beings, but we belong to the same club."

"Yep, but I haven't found anything like what we have."

"Which means we have an ability never before known, at least according to these books."

I closed my book. "I don't think we need to do any more research."

"I agree. We've learned all we're going to learn."

"Our telepathy is different. We are different."

"Unique. The last thing we wanted to be."

We gathered all the books and slowly, methodically placed them back in the stacks, and returned the room key to the librarian on duty. Not the one with leopard yoga pants and manicured nails because she'd long since gone home.

The current one was elderly and resembled librarians in books, with gray hair in a bun, sneakers, and a homemade lace collar on a dress so elegant I suspected it originated in Paris. Or possibly she was a very good seamstress. She, too, waved a friendly goodbye as we exited the building into a warm summer night.

We took a several block detour through a somewhat busy business section looking for a fast food place with the intention of doing what we did coming, except in reverse. Eating on the road. When we found one, we got hamburgers and pop. I settled back in my seat and prepared to enjoy the ride and a meal as Tate threaded through the labyrinthine streets towards the freeway.

He waited patiently through a stop light, but when it turned green, instead of heading for the freeway as I expected, he turned into a residential area. At the first corner, he turned again, went down a street filled with single family homes and parked cars, and then turned still again into an area of apartment buildings.

"Are you taking the scenic route?" A casual question but the thrumming had begun deep in me, subtle but strong and this time it was scary. I couldn't push it away and knew the sensation had come from Tate. Because we were somehow joined.

"Just being cautious." The thrumming increased.

"About what?" I saw nothing.

"A couple more turns in this mess of neighborhoods, and I'll know if I'm right or just being paranoid."

"Tell me!" The thrumming was strong enough to make me feel like I was shaking though I wasn't. Not physically anyway.

"There was a dark car. It left the library at the same time we did. When we turned into the business district, it did too. When we left the fast food place and headed for the freeway, it went in the same direction. It could be coincidence. Food then heading for home is common. They could be doing the same thing we are. But it always kept few cars behind us, and that made me suspicious."

"They are following us?"

"I don't know. That's why I'm taking the long way to the freeway. If they take the same route we are we'll know they are following us because no one would normally take this circuitous kind of route."

I went silent as Tate concentrated on driving. Not too fast, obeying all laws, but watching the rear view mirror.

Eventually, we reached the freeway and merged with the traffic heading out of town. I craned my neck to see behind us, but it was night and Tate had said the car was dark. "Most of the cars are dark."

"It's probably gone." His hands on the steering wheel eased their grip. "It was most likely my imagination." He grabbed his hamburger. It was cold but he didn't seem to notice. "I'm hyper after what happened at the library and am seeing conspiracies where there aren't any."

"Or maybe there are, and you saw what was actually there."

The drive home was quiet. When we reached the Cape Cod, Noble let us know we'd been gone far too long, but he must have forgiven me because his tail didn't stop wagging and he stuck to me like glue.

We didn't talk about the incident at the library, or the car that might have been following us, but they hung over us until we went to bed. I thought about them for a long time as I readied for the night while Noble curled onto his usual spot on my bed.

I wasn't used to cloak and dagger stuff. I wasn't used to telepathy. Too many things, I decided, as I rolled onto my side and pulled a blanket tight. My life was becoming way too complicated. But there wasn't any way to turn back the time to before I stopped at the overlook.

CHAPTER 8

The next morning started normally enough, considering it was a new normal that included a man sleeping upstairs who was turning my fixer-upper into a livable house whom I could communicate with mentally. Add to that the fact that I was going to have to fight against how he turned me into mush just by existing, which could also be part of the new normal and was probably temporary, though it didn't feel temporary. It was all very confusing.

But Noble was my old normal, and I was grateful for him. He gobbled breakfast before disappearing though the doggie door to whatever adventure was on his agenda for that day, but he did so only after letting me know with his best and most practiced sad doggie expression that he'd been alone the day before, and was I sorry for abandoning him? If not, his face said, I should be. Then he was gone.

Tate came downstairs soon after Noble disappeared, taking the stairs two at a time in his usual, cheerful morning persona. I shuddered at the very thought of such cheerfulness so early, took another slug of strong, black coffee in the hope it would raise my morning doldrums enough to meet him halfway, and pasted on a lopsided smile. "What's on your agenda today?"

"The upstairs door trim."

"Is there a problem?" I'd not got around to investigating the upstairs since moving in. Too many other fixer-upper type problems for it to be a priority.

"It's not bad but it's not square either. I'll check it out today, see what can be done, and add it to my list." He passed me on his way to the refrigerator where he pulled out bacon and eggs and started cooking, giving me a lopsided smile that was wider, brighter, and in all ways better than my smile. A lot better. Real, not forced. "I've noticed you aren't into cooking in the morning. I'll make breakfast."

"You cook?"

"When necessary, and I've noticed mornings don't seem to be your best time." I subsided into a chair and proceeded to watch him work while I did nothing at all beyond drink more coffee and slowly acknowledge that it was going to be a gorgeous day with the sun filtering through the trees and the birds fighting to drown each other out. He dumped bacon into the frying pan and asked, "Where's Noble?"

"On his usual morning expedition." I shrugged and breathed in hot coffee fumes mixed with the smell of bacon. "I never know where he goes, but I have no close neighbors, and he can handle himself in the forest, so I don't worry about him."

At which moment Noble reappeared through his doggie door and went straight to the stove and Tate and begged for bacon. Or eggs. Or anything edible. Tate sneaked a look at me. Seeing I was seemingly lost in coffee fumes, he dropped a piece of bacon to the floor, except it was snapped up by my greedy dog in mid-air.

"I saw that."

"He looked hungry."

Noble moved closer to Tate, hoping for a repeat of the bacon. But before he moved two steps he stopped. His ears went up and the hair on his back rose. His tail went down, and he went through to the living room and approached the door, teeth not quite bared but close. He growled low. He left no doubt that something was wrong.

Tate followed. "What does he see?"

I was spooked after the library incident. I carefully looked through the kitchen window but saw nothing. Tate chose the living room window and peered one way and another, then at Noble, but my dog still stood at attention, ears pricked as he listened to something we couldn't hear.

Then we heard it and I sagged in relief. "A car. Someone is coming. He scared me." I returned to my chair with a fresh cup of hot coffee and breathed in more fumes.

"Do you have a lot of visitors?"

"I'm somewhat of a recluse so I don't get a lot, but it happens occasionally."

Tate stayed at the window, far enough back to not be easily visible but watching the car as it turned into the driveway. "Know anyone with a black car?"

Dread crept into my stomach. "Is it the car from last night?"

"I didn't get a good look at it. But it could be."

A car door slammed and footsteps approached. Soon there was a knock on the door. Tate looked at me. "Want me to answer?"

I stood up. "It's my house. My company. My

responsibility."

Tate looked at Noble, who was still on alert. "You answer then, but I'll be nearby." In case whoever was knocking was dangerous.

I almost puked. Instead, I motioned to Noble, who went to the kitchen when I pointed to it because I didn't want a visitor to be greeted by growls and bared teeth. Noble didn't want to be shut away, but he accepted his fate and settled on the floor near the door to the living room.

I answered the door and saw a middle-aged man in a suit and tie that was totally out of place in the wilderness. That alone sent shivers along my spine.

"Are you Zoe Smith?" I nodded and waited. "My name is Mike Dickens. I'd like to ask a few questions if you don't mind. If you have the time." He smiled perfunctorily. "I'm here about what happened."

"What are you talking about?"

Was he here because his black car didn't catch us? Because we hoarded all the books on the supernatural? I didn't for a second think he'd come for any reason other than the library visit. Or the telepathy. Or the vortex.

"May I come in?"

I glanced at Tate who nodded imperceptibly though he was on high alert, something Mike Dickens noticed while pretending not to. But Tate's unfriendly expression didn't stop him or even slow him down. He entered without waiting for me to answer, but he kept an eye on Tate and gave him a wide berth.

Tate stared at Mike with his best alpha male expression and gave the impression Mike had his full focus, but he spoke to my mind loud and clear. "*Let him come in. Let's find out what this is about."*

Mike looked Tate up and down much like a personnel manager might while interviewing a potential employee he'd already decided not to hire. "You must be Tate Brewster." He knew who Tate was. That shook me up. "I'm glad to see you here. Saves me a second visit because what I have to say is for both of you."

I didn't offer Mike a chair but he sat anyway, on the couch in the most central place in the living room.

I was grateful for the telepathy. We could talk without this Mike person knowing. *"What's going on?"*

"I don't know but don't let him get to you. Don't be intimidated."

"How can I not be? He barged in and is acting like he owns the place."

"It's a tactic. He deliberately chose the most central place to sit. A subtle show of strength that'll only work if you let it."

Tate's eyes narrowed. He remained standing, arms crossed, feet apart, as he spoke out loud. "I can't imagine what you have to say that involves both of us."

Before replying, Mike examined his feet, shod in expensive black leather shoes. The kind you see in executive suites. Then his look moved to Tate and me in our rough clothes more suited to life in the country but way less expensive. *"Another tactic to make us feel inferior, which means he's well trained in intimidation. Ignore it."*

I followed Tate's lead. I said nothing and pretended I didn't know what Mike was doing. I dropped as casually as I could manage onto the chair nearest the kitchen and folded my hands in my lap. Tate eyed me from his post a few feet away. Mike didn't try to hide his appreciation of my silent declaration that we wouldn't be intimidated, which meant Tate was right. It had been a deliberate intimidation tactic and he recognized that I knew what he was doing.

Mike dropped the intimidation tactics and leaned forward in a confidential manner. Tate didn't blink, but he did message me telepathically. *"Don't be fooled. He's not giving up. He's merely changing tactics. He's now pretending to treat us as equals in whatever game he's playing, but don't for a second think it's anything other than another ruse."*

Mike's hands fluttered as he leaned still closer. "There are security cameras at the nearby rest area." I somehow managed not to react. "So we know you two were at the overlook when what I've been told was a substantial wind came up the canyon."

Tate nodded. "We were there."

"It was quite a nasty blow. The overlook had to be closed, and crews are still cleaning up. I've been sent to see if you two are okay. People are quite concerned about your welfare."

"And whether we plan to sue."

Mike cringed. Pretended to cringe. "I wouldn't blame you if you do."

"We won't."

Mike pretended to relax. "Glad to hear, but I do have a few questions if you two have a moment." All polite and not in the least genuine.

Tate moved until he was behind my chair and rested his hands on the back. Another tactic, one that didn't need an explanation. We were together for whatever we'd do. A team, a pair, fully united in our response to this visit.

"It's true we were at the overlook, and it's also true that a nasty wind came, but we saw it coming in time to duck between those two huge rocks. We were safe and are fine."

"So that's how come you weren't hurt." Mike pretended to be relieved. "When we saw that large branches had been thrown about and realized from security camera footage that you two must been at the overlook when it happened, we were concerned. You could have been hit by something. You could have sustained serious injuries."

"We didn't. We're fine. So you can tell whoever sent you that we were safe and have no plans to sue anyone." Tate moved his hands close enough that they touched me lightly. "I'm sorry you came all this way for nothing but, as you can see, we are unhurt."

We waited for Mike to leave. Instead he leaned back, folded his hands, and settled in. "I have a few more questions. If you don't mind, of course. If you have time."

I wanted this man gone. "Does it matter if we don't?"

"Great comment!" There was laughter in Tate's telepathic voice. *"Don't let him get to you."* Then he added, *"But keep him thinking we actually believe the crap he's giving us."*

"Will he believe nothing happened to us?"

"Not likely, but he has to pretend this is a normal conversation and that he's here only because someone truly cares about our welfare."

Mike sighed hugely. It was so fake I almost laughed and would have if not for Tate's hand on my shoulder. "In a way it doesn't matter if you want me here or not. Sorry, but these questions must be asked. And answered." He sank deeper into the couch, a gesture that plainly said he wasn't moving until he got the information he came for. "Insurance companies want to know all kinds of unnecessary things."

"He'll find out what happened."

"He doesn't know everything. If he did, he wouldn't be here. All we have to do is say it was just a really big wind and that's all we know and then keep saying it until we wear him out and he leaves."

At that moment, I was glad Noble was part of my life. He'd politely stayed in the kitchen while Mike talked, but it wasn't possible for him to be good forever. As Mike settled deep into the couch, Noble decided to join us in the living room where he sank onto the rug in front of me and stared at Mike. Just stared, but his doggie stare was more intimidating than any of the human variety.

Noble, being a rather large dog, had the added advantage of size when he bared his teeth and raised his fur, and he did both as he stared at my visitor. I was sure his wagging tail that normally indicated friendliness was intentional and intended to throw Mike off guard by presenting both good and bad vibes. Good dog and bad dog. Noble should be in Hollywood. He was a great actor.

"Does your dog bite?"

"Only on command."

"Is that true? Will Noble attack?"

"It's a total bluff. Like when the kids tried to rob us. You bluffed and it would have worked if not for their leader."

Tate's mental laughter was loud and delighted.

"Look at Mike. I believe he's afraid of Noble. Unlike my bluff, his might work."

Mike Dickens lost some of his composure as he carefully pulled his expensively shod feet closer to his body. He truly was uncomfortable with Noble in the room. I considered sending my dog back to the kitchen. Instead, I scratched his ears so he'd know he was a good dog.

But, as seconds passed without incident, Mike relaxed once more and returned to the subject at hand. The incident at the overlook. "Are you sure the wind didn't affect you in some way? Something not physically harmful but concerning nevertheless?"

"He knows something."

"I wish we could ask questions."

"Don't!"

"I won't. I just wish I could."

"He's fishing. All we have to do is wait him out. He'll leave when he realizes he won't get anything from us."

That proved true. After a few more questions while watching Noble with his peripheral vision, Mike rose and headed for the door. "Well, I guess there's nothing more to be done here." He handed us each a business card. "My contact information in case you remember something. After effects. Delayed reactions. Anything. We'll take care of any and all problems arising from the wind. Call me and I promise to personally deal with them."

He left. We watched his car disappear in a cloud of dust. I turned back to Noble, led him into the kitchen, and gave him a doggie treat. "Because you were such a good boy." He wagged his tail in thanks.

Tate watched, head tilted and thumbs hooked through his belt. "Good boy indeed. If Noble didn't already have a human, I'd bid for the job."

Then he proved he was ahead of me. "It's still morning. What say we head to the lookout and see what Mike was talking about?"

"That they are cleaning up debris?"

"Maybe we'll learn something. About what happened, or about this Mike guy who I wouldn't trust as far as I could throw a cement block the size of Noble."

CHAPTER 9

We didn't take Noble when we went to check out the rest stop. His feelings were hurt when he saw we were leaving still again without him but he was consoled with left-over bacon we hadn't gotten around to eating because Mike Dickens interrupted breakfast.

The rest stop was a busy place. Not travelers taking a break from driving, though there were a few of those. Most of the spaces were occupied by local cars and trucks. When we walked to the rest stop building, we saw a handful of people hanging around the vending machines. Men, mostly. Workers by the look of them. Work clothes, heavy boots, and hard hats.

We left the main building and headed for the path to the overlook, but were stopped by a barricade. We looked as far down the path as we could see. The overlook itself wasn't in sight, but we saw the top of a crane where it should be and heard the buzz of chain saws. When we went to the road used by maintenance vehicles to reach the overlook, we saw a truck loaded with tree parts. We stepped aside as it passed and stared. The sign that told what people were looking at, the history of the view was also in the truck. "It's new and looks okay. It doesn't need replacing."

"Looks like Mike was telling the truth when he

said some work is being done. What he didn't say was how much work. This is a lot."

We returned to the main building where the workers had finished their break. We approached them. "We see the overlook is closed. We're disappointed. We were hoping to see the valley. We were told the view is spectacular so we're wondering how long it will take to do whatever you guys are doing. Maybe we can stick around until you finish."

One of the workers shook his head. "Sorry, but you won't be able to go there. Not now or ever."

Another finished his pop and tossed the can into the recycle bin. "We're not just cleaning up. Our orders are to demolish it and return it to its previous wild state."

That was a shock. "We heard there was a storm that did some damage. I can see why that would need to be cleared away. But was it so bad that the overlook is beyond repair?"

A third man joined in. "The clean-up was easy. There was a lot of stuff tossed around by the wind but not much worse than with any bad storm. Branches, leaves, and twigs all over the place, and some trees were knocked over. But the overlook itself withstood the wind. As it was designed to do."

"Then why demolish it? We're from out of state and made a detour here just to see what all the fuss is about. It's kind of a landmark in this part of the country, so I'm surprised someone decided to eliminate it."

Tate glanced at the parking lot and the cars with out of state license plates. "I'd think anything so well-known would be an asset worth keeping."

The man who'd spoken last shrugged. "I long ago gave up trying to second guess those in power. It makes no sense at all because you are right, it's a beautiful view, and this rest stop is always busy and, with the overlook gone, most people will cruise on by without stopping."

The shortest of the group was a middle-aged man with muscles hard from years of physical work. From the way the others deferred to him, he was the boss. Now he chimed in. "From what I heard, it wasn't politicians who made the decision, and I'm pretty sure they didn't decide to destroy it for political reasons because it brought people to the area. Instead, I heard they made the decision after a visit by a couple guys from the research facility at the bottom of the valley."

"There's a research place down there?" I pretended surprise. "What do they do?"

"No one knows. They are a pretty close-mouthed bunch, and not the friendly type." The middle-aged man shook his head. "You know how it goes. If you get lost and drive up to the facility to ask directions, they'll greet you with guns and nasty expressions. So, to my knowledge, no one ever asked questions. They just turned around and got out of there as fast as they could."

"So the research facility is behind the overlook being closed?"

"That's what we hear." The middle-aged man crushed his empty pop can with one hand and indicated a huge blonde man in work clothes and a hard hat heading their way. "Boss is watching and break time is over so we'd better get back to work." He started for the path to the overlook, followed by his crew.

We were left staring at the trail and the barricade that blocked it. "I wish we could see what they're doing. Not that it'll help with our problem. I just want to know for sure that it's gone."

"We can go around the barricade."

"We'd be stopped before we got two feet past it." The crew disappeared around a bend in the trail. "Besides, we don't have to see what's being done, because we know."

Tate flexed his arms. "I want to check it out. It could be important someday down the line. Think of it as extra insurance. The more we know the better we can plan our next step."

"You assume we need a plan."

Tate was grim. "We might."

I examined the area. "My neighbor, the one who had the road made in the woods because he can't walk well anymore, said there's a path somewhere around here that went to the overlook before it was an overlook. He used to go there all the time before the state made it nice and pretty with a fence and everything. The walk to a lovely place was what got him wanting his own road through his woods."

"Do you think it still exists?"

"He told me approximately where it used to be."

We walked along the grass between the rest area and the forest. We crossed the road that was used to transport heavy equipment to the overlook for maintenance but ignored it, along with the discreet trail crews used to avoid crowds during the busy summer season. And eventually we found what was left of the original path my neighbor had described.

We looked back at the rest area. A handful of

people were eating at the tables scattered throughout the area, and a couple cars were leaving, and new ones were arriving. A few people were entering the main building. But no one was looking our way, so we stepped over the concrete divider between the rest area and the thick forest. And disappeared.

It was clear the trail hadn't been used in a long time. It was overgrown and crisscrossed with roots and dead branches. But if we went slowly and carefully we could make out the general direction, and sooner than we'd thought possible we sighted clear skies ahead that meant we were almost there.

The sound of machinery wasn't enough to drown out the shouts of workers. *"Lots of people."* Without discussion, we'd switched to telepathy. *"And they're in a hurry."*

"Their bosses are eager to get rid of the evidence."

"I don't like that idea. We are evidence."

"Which is most likely why Mike Dickens showed up at your place this morning." I shivered. What would have happened if we'd told him what had happened to us?

We crept close enough to see what was going on. The place was unrecognizable as the overlook we'd visited recently. Earth movers had clawed the ground away almost to the forest edge, and it was obvious that was their intention. They were moving the huge rocks Tate and I had sheltered between, pulling them towards the empty space while making sure to keep them upright. When they were in place they'd stand between the forest and the cliff. There'd be no place for anyone to stand while looking over the valley except by climbing the rocks, and their sides were so sheer that was unlikely.

"They definitely don't want anyone to hang around and enjoy the view."

"It was a beautiful place. People loved to come here."

"Not any more."

I shivered. Tate moved close and wrapped his arms around me. *"There are other beautiful places. The world is full of them."*

"I don't know those places. I know this place. It's one of the reasons I decided to live here."

His arms tightened and he pulled me close. His chest was warm and solid and reassuring enough that the shivering stopped and I freed myself, feeling more than a little foolish, but he said, *"It's normal to grieve the end of such a nice place."*

I sucked in my breath. *"How'd you know what I was thinking?"* Though I knew how. The weird thing that was more than telepathy that I sometimes thought didn't exist, and other times, like now, knew was real.

"Grieving when you lose something precious is normal, and you lost something that was special to you." He looked past my shoulder and stiffened. *"Someone's coming."*

We backed behind a tree and went still. We saw someone heading back towards the rest area along the path used by the workers. Not a worker, though, this man wore a suit and moved like someone in charge. We peered through thick pine needles. *"It's Mike Dickens."*

"And someone with him."

Mike followed a larger man who walked with a longer, more important stride. *"Mike's boss?"*

"The man behind what happened to us?"

They didn't see us. Didn't look to either side of the path. *"They're in a hurry."*

"Let's see where they go."

We followed slowly and with caution so as not to be seen, but there was no danger of losing them because the only place they could go was the rest stop. We emerged from the forest in time to see them cross the parking lot and get into a dark car that was parked alongside the cars and trucks belonging to the workers.

"There's a logo on the side, but I can't read it from here." The driver backed out with the abruptness that denotes anger, but he merged smoothly onto the freeway where its fast pace wouldn't call attention to it.

We followed the walkway to the area set aside for the workers' vehicles. They were personal vehicles, but when we went past them to a few additional cars, those additional black cars had the same logos as the one we'd just seen pull away. WFA Inc.

"What's that stand for?"

I pulled out my cell phone and snapped a picture of the logo. Then we went into the main building and pretended to look through the flyers in the inevitable display, after which we approached the man behind the counter. "Can you help us?"

His shift had just started. He was wide awake, and attentive, and cordial. He smiled in a professionally friendly way. "I can try."

"We're wondering who's demolishing the overlook. What company was hired."

"I believe the facility at the bottom of the valley offered to do the job. For free, so they got the contract."

"We were talking with some of the workers. I got the impression they are recent hires."

"I was told this is a bigger job than their usual work load, so they did hire some outside help, but you'd have to ask them to be sure."

"That's very generous of them to do it for free. Do you happen to know the name of the facility?"

"Weather For America."

"Sounds interesting. What exactly do they do?"

His face fell. "I'm afraid I don't know." He wanted to be helpful. "Maybe they are a weather station? Data and stuff like that?"

We thanked hm and left. "He didn't know much."

"We know the name of the facility and, with that name, it stands to reason that they have something to do with weather. We already know we are telepathic because of a wind that came from the valley. That's weather, and their facility is where the wind was born."

"So we do more research, only this time we find out about WFA."

"If it's as secretive as people say, it won't be easy."

"There's got to be a way."

Tate was silent for a long time. Then he said, "I have an idea though it might not work."

"What kind of idea?"

"I might know someone who can help." Then he added, "If he will. Billy's a good friend but even he has limits, and who knows what we'll be getting into when we start investigating a company that values secrecy above all else."

"Can he find out about WFA?"

"We'll find out as much as we can ourselves. Then I'll contact Billy and ask if he can find out the stuff that's not for public consumption."

CHAPTER 10

We didn't go straight home. Tate took a detour. "I passed this place on my way here. I didn't know there was a public overlook in the area, so when I saw what seemed like a nice vista, I stopped." He turned off the road onto a grassy area and parked. "You can no longer visit the overlook you like but maybe this can be a substitute."

He knew how sad I was about the overlook being demolished. He felt it. Somehow.

I followed him to the edge of a hill overlooking a valley every bit as awesome as the one we'd just left. Because the area was full of them. No dramatic cliff with a valley at the bottom, instead this vista spread over uncounted miles of forested hills dotted with so many lakes I couldn't count them all. "It's breathtaking." The space in me that mourned the loss of the overlook filled with this new view of the forested region so I said the only thing I could say. "Thank you."

We gave ourselves a few minutes to commune with nature and then continued home. Noble was waiting with a wagging tail and proceeded to lick us both to death. "Tate, you're getting as much attention as I am, so he must now consider you family."

Tate considered the large Lab ruefully. "I'm flattered. I think."

"He has discriminating taste. Remember how he threatened to eat Mike Dickens? As was appropriate? Now he's loving you to pieces, as is also appropriate."

After Noble decided he'd loved us sufficiently, we headed for my computer and looked up Weather For America. "They provide weather forecasts for farmers and the like. People whose jobs depend on knowing what's coming before it comes. They claim their forecasts are so specific they can predict the weather for an individual farm or work site."

"Nothing sinister in that."

I pointed to the web page. "It's the right WFA. Their logo is the same as the ones at the overlook." But something about the site was off. Wrong.

It was Tate who figured it out. "Weather For America is headquartered thousands of miles away. Like half a continent away." A map showed their service area. "Nothing even remotely close to here."

"The facility here could be a satellite office. A mini station monitoring the weather for a while to help those in power decide if they should move into this area."

"Or it could be a true research facility like everyone says, only one that does really bizarre experiments. I go with that explanation because the locals think it, and locals always know more than people in power give them credit for."

Noble came and went as we checked out WFA, but each time he joined us he let us know we were working too hard. It was a lovely day outside. Lots of squirrels to chase, birds to bark at, mysterious scents to investigate, and he shouldn't have to do those things alone.

I petted Noble in the hope he'd learn patience as I read reviews of WFA and checked out the business. "They seem reputable, and everyone says they deliver on their promises. So they truly are a weather-related business."

"No complaints. No fraud. Nothing out of the ordinary. Just a no-nonsense weather forecasting company that's been around as long as pin-point weather forecasting has existed."

"Farmers love WFA. So do construction companies. Some have been customers for years. But the company has never gone beyond their coastal origins. Until now."

"So why are they here?"

Noble woofed so loud that we couldn't ignore him. "He won't give up until he has a walk."

Tate stroked the big Lab and agreed. "He's one big bundle of energy."

I closed the laptop and looked for the dog leash. "I like to take it with me in case he gets wanderlust. I may have to forcibly haul him back."

"Can I come? Maybe together we can keep him under control. Besides I think better when I'm doing something, and I've hit a brick wall with WFA. Maybe a little physical activity will jar my brains loose."

So, accompanied by one ecstatic black Labrador retriever, we set off. "My neighbor's road begins just past the house. Noble is used to taking walks along it and he knows to stay on the road, so he won't stray as much if we walk there than if we go through the forest itself."

We'd had a lot of rain. The green stuff grew thicker

every day. I was glad for the path I'd cleared from the Cape Cod to the forest road so I didn't have to get wet plowing through bushes to reach it. Once we reached the road, though, it was clear and easy to walk because my neighbor's caretaker kept it meticulously clean for the four wheeler that was the only vehicle ever on it. I was the only person besides him who used along it. "You're the second," I told Tate who was busy watching Noble chase a chipmunk off the road.

"It's quiet here," Tate said after Noble gave up on cornering the chipmunk. "Not a twig, and there's enough brush on either side to muffle sounds." I explained for the second time about the well-maintained road, and he merely said, "If the four-wheeler is electric there's no way anyone would guess this road exists." I agreed and slowed even more because he was right about the quiet, and I wanted to enjoy it more. I welcomed it.

Then we heard something. Nothing we could identify, but the past few days had made both of us paranoid. *"Shhhh,"* Tate said mentally. *"Let's stop so we can figure out what it is."* Noble was a ways ahead. Now he turned back and wanted to know why we weren't keeping up with him. He was clearly irritated. *"Is there a way to keep him quiet?"*

"I can try. But you know Noble." Tate's eyeroll said he did indeed know my independent dog.

I gestured towards Noble, and he responded by bounding back to me, knowing I had treats in my pocket because I always had treats. I brought out a doggie biscuit and gave it to him. I also stroked his back and stooped low to pay even more attention to him because he loved people who loved him, and he promptly responded to this unusual attention by sitting on his rump and asking to be petted even more.

As Noble and I sat in the middle of the road, Tate moved towards the sound. There was no danger of his giving away our presence because of the groomed road but he chose each step with care anyway, taking longer than necessary to reach the edge. Then he stood still and indicated that I should do the same. I hugged Noble and the dog quieted down even more. His eyes half closed, and he lay down and rolled over on his back. I scratched his belly, and he went as still as Tate and I.

The sound was faint, but it was unmistakably human. *"No one else lives even remotely nearby. Just my neighbor and me, and he's in a wheelchair so it's not him."*

"A relative of his perhaps? A visitor?"

"He has no relatives and, like me, he's kind of a hermit. That's a lot of the reason we get along well. We are alike in that way."

Tate nodded that he'd got my nonverbal messages. Then he proceeded to leave the road and thread his way through the forest itself towards the sound. One step at a time, examining the forest floor before him and choosing the clearest area to place each step while keeping thick tree trunks between him and whomever was making the sound. *"This could take a while."*

"We're good here. Noble is going to sleep."

Tate disappeared. One second I could see his stealthy progress, and the next he was gone. *"Are you okay? I can't see you."*

"I'm good. I know I'm slow but I'm getting closer. I can hear actual voices now instead of just vague sounds. I'm guessing they are men, at least two, though

it's hard to tell how many."

"What are they saying?"

"I can't hear that yet. Soon."

"I'm thankful for the telepathy thing. I'd go crazy if I had to stay here with Noble without knowing what's happening."

"I'll keep you informed."

I strained to hear what was happening, but there was nothing beyond a murmur I couldn't make out, so I settled down to pet Noble and wait for more information to be transferred mentally through the telepathy that by now felt almost normal.

"I'm done here. I'm on my way back." Tate's mental speech was almost jarring after sitting quietly with Noble.

"Did you learn anything?"

"Enough that I want to concentrate solely on not being heard. I'll tell you about it when we get home. Right now, getting through the forest is tricky. It's getting late." Not late according to the clock but dusk came early where trees grew thick and tall and the sun could only penetrate their foliage for a brief time each day.

When I saw him through the trees I rose as quietly as possible and snapped Noah's leash on the sleeping dog. I'd wait as long as possible before waking him.

I took one look at Tate's grim face and gently woke the sleeping dog, bending close and stroking his forehead as he came awake to forestall any noises he might make. Then I rose. When Noble was fully awake, Tate moved down the forest road and Noble and I followed. We went slowly at first because silence was essential, but as we moved far enough away from whomever Tate had seen through the trees to be reasonably sure we wouldn't be heard, we sped up until we were stepping out as fast as we could.

We returned to the Cape Cod in less than half the time it had taken to leave, and I made sure Noble came inside. Then I locked his doggie door. No sense taking the chance of him wandering away and visiting whomever Tate had seen.

I made coffee and steered us to the porch when it was ready. There'd been no talk of any kind, verbal or telepathic, since arriving home, but the time had come for answers.

Tate sank into one of the porch chairs and took a sip. "It was as I thought. Two men." Another sip, then he said, "And two cars."

The way he said it brought a tightness to my throat. "Were they dark?"

"Black as sin and with logos on them."

I wanted to puke. "WFA logos?"

He nodded, breathing in the hot steam. "Exactly."

"Did you hear what they said?"

He shook his head. "I didn't dare get any closer. Too many twigs on the ground. They'd have heard me for sure. So I didn't get their words." He formed his hands around the cup as people do when they are cold, though it was a warm day. "But I know what they were doing."

"What?" I reached for my own coffee.

"Watching your house."

The coffee scalded my throat, but I barely noticed. "How do you know?"

"They pointed in this direction several times, and they were arguing. One man seemed to be in charge, and I believe he wanted the other to move closer to your house, but the second man disagreed vehemently, probably because he thought he'd be seen if he was any closer." I wrapped my own hands around my cup. I knew how Tate had felt when he'd done the same. In need of warmth and security. "Finally, the man in charge stomped away in anger, got in his car, and peeled out of there like the devil was after him."

"What did the other man do then?"

"Nothing. He just turned to look towards your house. He couldn't see it, of course, but I bet if we were standing where he's standing and looked in this direction, we'd be able to see anyone near your house and that was why he was there. To see well enough to know what we're doing."

I hugged Noble. Hard. Tate watched somberly. "Which means it's time to leave."

I agreed. "You should go. Be safe."

"Not just me. Us. Both of us. We should both get out of here while we still can."

"I can't just up and leave. It's my home."

"It's not safe. Not any more. I'm leaving but I'm not going without you." He put his coffee down and leaned towards me. "Think about it. We don't know who these people are other than that they profess to be part of WFA. We don't know what they think happened to us back there at the overlook, but they know something happened.

"Furthermore, we don't know what their plans for us are." He took a deep breath and stared at me hard. "But we do know they have plans of some kind, and I doubt their plans are to make nice."

I put my cup down and hugged my waist. His

words hurt bad, but they were true. "They want to experiment on us."

"Or worse."

I shivered. "Where can we go?"

"We'll figure it out."

"So far away that there's not even a tiny chance they can find us."

"Far away and preferably off the map."

"Where is that?"

"I might know a place. Not for sure and I'll have to do some checking, but even if it doesn't pan out we still are getting out of here as soon as possible. We have no alternative. Even if we have to take what we can carry and drive until we run out of gas."

I sank deep into my chair and wished I'd never gone to that overlook. A week ago I'd never in my wildest dreams have believed I'd now be considering leaving the home and life I'd so carefully created.

CHAPTER 11

I didn't sleep that night and was glad for it because ,without sleep, I had no nightmares. But in the morning, I had a thousand questions. "You knew those things yesterday because you were in the military. Weren't you?" He nodded. "So you know about stuff like this. Scary stuff, and you know what to do? How to do it?"

He hooked a foot around a chair and dragged it out enough to sit so we stared at one another across the kitchen table. "In the military I learned how to shoot a gun and march more miles than any reasonable human should ever do, and a lot of other stuff. Some of it was helpful, most of it wasn't. I learned the other stuff simply by living."

"But you have a plan. Don't you?"

"Maybe, but I need to go to town before I can say for sure."

"Why?" If it was essential he go because our safety depended on it then so be it, but my face said I was concerned.

"Do you want to come with me?"

"Do you want me to come?"

He licked his lips and finally shook his head. "I want you to stay here so the guy who's watching us doesn't get suspicious. But staying could be dangerous for you." I felt his indecision. "I don't want to put you in danger but I might need to go away several times. I want him to think it's a normal thing for me to do. But each time I'm gone can be dangerous for you."

"Stop trying to protect me. I have that Glock, remember, and I know how to use it. Besides, if my car hadn't died, we'd have gone our separate ways and I'd be alone anyway."

"It still bothers me."

"I have Noble. He's a great big love bug, but I feel sorry for anyone who interferes with his life. Or his food. Or me."

"Keep him close."

Tate eyed the huge Lab and the two connected. I knew what they were thinking. In spite of my insisting I could handle my life, they were going to protect me and they were totally serious as they stared at one another. Two guys protecting their female. I would have laughed if things weren't so dire.

"What are you going to do in town?"

"The first thing will be to buy a burner phone." The silent laughter that had bubbled up at the thought of my two protectors died instantly. We could be traced through our phones. What else did we need to do that hadn't occurred to me that Tate was already planning? "The second thing will be to check on your car repairs."

"Because two vehicles will be better than one?"

"Two will carry more stuff. Food. Whatever else we can take."

"Because there might not be supplies where we're going?"

He nodded. "We shouldn't use credit cards because

they can be traced. I have a fair amount of cash on me now, but it won't last forever."

I sobered still more. "I can empty my account in town. My main funds aren't there though. I inherited stock from my great-aunt so I get dividends every so often, but my financial manager is half way across the country."

"Good. Let them accumulate. They'll be there when this is over, but they can paint a target on you now."

I stared at my coffee. How'd I been able to drink it earlier? I couldn't swallow anything now. "The repair guy said my car might take a few days."

"Maybe I can motivate him to get it done faster."

"Don't hurt him."

Tate laughed. The sound broke the tension that had been building. "I was thinking more along the lines of a bribe." Relief flowed through me, and I hoped he didn't know what I'd been thinking. "From now on cash is precious and I hope I don't have to use too much of it, but I only use physical persuasion when someone is trying to rob us."

Us. As if we were a team. A pair. A joined couple. Which made me wonder which we were and, somehow, he knew what I was thinking. His eyes went dark. "A couple. That's what we are. I don't know about you, but that's what it feels like to me."

Our looks met then slid away because we'd agreed not to go down that path. Too much else to deal with. But whatever was between us felt more solid than ever after his words. I just wished I knew what the future would bring. But telepathy wasn't precognition.

Tate headed for town. We made a big show of his

leaving for the watcher's sake. I said how much I'd miss him as loudly as I could in case the watcher was close enough to hear. Before climbing into his truck, Tate casually leaned in close and kissed me. It was for show, not for real, but the effect on me was as genuine as if it was real and Tate was similarly affected. I knew he was. I felt it in him.

"I'll be back. Today if possible, tomorrow at the latest." We scrambled to recover from the kiss and continue our play-acting. "Sure you'll be okay here alone?"

"I'll be fine." I reached up and kissed him again. A goodbye kiss, like anyone would do, and again I had to remind myself afterwards to breathe, and I wasn't alone in that. Tate, also, was affected. Again, I knew he was, and he knew how I felt, too, and I'd never experienced that with anyone else. The knowing was weird and somehow wonderful and I vowed to explore it when there was time.

The telepathy was wonderful because we kept in constant contact while he was gone. *"Any problem with our new, hidden, and unwanted spy?"*

"He's staying out of sight."

"I was afraid if I left, he'd come after you."

"Nope."

"Good. Now I can head for town."

"You should be half-way there by now."

"I pulled over as soon as I turned a corner so I could return immediately if he decided to be nasty."

"I've told you before. I can handle myself."

"I know. The Glock."

"That and Noble. He truly is a guard dog when he's in the mood."

Tate's chuckle was as loud and clear in my mind as was his determination to keep me safe. He was the alpha male in spades protecting the nearest fragile female. Except I wasn't fragile, something he didn't seem to understand.

But even as he drove to town and I stayed in the Cape Cod, he knew the direction of my thoughts. Knew them and acknowledged them as truth. Yes, he was a bit over-protective, he said, and maybe someday he'd change. Maybe.

Then he concentrated on driving, and I turned to cleaning the Cape Cod until he returned because it was physical and required no thought or emotion. I wasn't capable of either.

I was amazed at how quickly I'd gotten used to having him in my house and in my life. He was a part of my daily routine now, and I sharply felt his absence.

We'd spent hours deciding on our course of action, but we hadn't gone beyond what the watcher should see. We didn't want him to check on me because I was alone, but neither did we want Tate's leaving to rouse his suspicions. The success of our plan depended on his thinking that our every move was normal. So I swept and dusted and polished the brass lamp in the corner and told myself that everything would be okay.

Tate returned at dusk, hopped out, and gave me another big kiss, lingering far longer than necessary. *"Think we fooled him?"*

"Maybe. If he's even looking, and we can't know that for sure without letting him know we're aware of him."

Tate kissed me a second time, taking longer this time. *"Let's make him a little envious. Give him something to think about."*

So I stood on my tiptoes and reached for Tate. *"I hope he's watching."*

Tate leaned into that kiss hard, and it lasted far longer than I'd planned, which was fine except for the fact that Tate knew how he was affecting me even as I knew I was doing the same to him.

"This lovey-dovey stuff is weird."

"It is indeed."

He pulled away, wrapped an arm around me, and practically dragged me inside. *"No more putting on a show for some sneaky idiot who's trying to become a big-time criminal."* As we went inside and he slammed the door, he added, *"Next time it won't be play-acting, but for now we have things to discuss."* And just like that what had been between us was gone and we were all business again.

Since we were inside, we spoke out loud, something we'd adapted to with surprising speed. Talking telepathically when there were people around and out loud when there weren't. It was becoming automatic and was just as weird in its own way as the little romantic scene we'd played out for someone who probably wasn't watching.

"Your car will be ready tomorrow."

"So soon?"

"The parts arrived and a small infusion of cash put you ahead of everyone else."

"I'll be glad to have it back."

"Don't bring it here."

"Why not?" That hadn't been part of the plan, at least not a part we'd talked over.

"Will your neighbor let you park it at his place?

The neighbor with the road through the woods?"

"I'm sure he will. He's a good neighbor. But why?"

"So the watcher won't know we have two vehicles. As far as he knows all we have is my truck. If things get nasty, we'll have a spare some place we can get to it." He paused. "Besides, with two vehicles we can carry more supplies."

"The pantry is full. Will that be enough?"

"We should use credit cards in town and buy as much as two vehicles will carry. Then we disappear and drop off the map by not buying anything except with cash and the amount of cash we have will be limited to what we can get from the bank in town."

He dropped into a comfortable chair. He looked years older than when we met. I probably did too. "Before we disappear we have to get as much as possible into the two vehicles without our friendly watcher being any the wiser."

"How?"

"I have some supplies in my truck that I bought in town, and we can sneak more into it tonight. I parked it as close to the house as possible without being obvious to lessen the possibility of being seen."

"What about my car?"

"We'll do the same thing only we'll do it at night. We'll park your car at your neighbor's house if he'll let us. It'll be harder to load it because we'll have to carry everything along your neighbor's wilderness road, and we'll have to do it without light and without being heard."

I tried to picture walking the road in the dark and failed. "That'll take forever."

"We'll work all night and sleep all day."

"Our spy will be suspicious if he doesn't see or hear us during the day."

"We'll turn on the TV and let Noble come and go through his doggie door so things will appear as normal as possible."

"It'll be hard, dark, and difficult."

"But worth it because once we are situated in a safe hideout we can hunker down and forget the world exists for as long as necessary."

"A hideout. Can we find such a place?"

"I told you before that I had an idea." His eyes gleamed. "I made a couple calls with my new burner phone, and it's all set."

CHAPTER 12

The next day we went to town together. I didn't close out my bank account though I was
tempted. It was smarter to do that on our way out of town. It would delay our departure, but we didn't want to be seen doing something suspicious too soon. We'd leave directly from the bank and hope the unusual action wasn't noticed.

While we were in town, I picked up my car from the repair shop. The repair man was all smiles and said it was as good as new.

But I didn't drive it home. Instead, Tate followed me to my neighbor's house where I asked if I could park my car there for a few days. He was okay with it. He was curious but too polite to ask questions and I didn't offer any explanations. I just thanked him politely as he agreed to my request. Then I parked it at the beginning of the forest road and left with Tate.

We'd loaded Tate's truck with groceries in town and made a great show of carrying some of them into the house when we returned to the Cape Cod but, once inside, instead of stocking the pantry we transferred everything to back packs and a garden cart that came with the house that I'd never used because I wasn't the gardening type. It was a large cart capable of carrying a small tree.

Tate greased the wheels and I oiled the handle until there was no possibility of even a single squeak. We sneaked the cart out the back door and hid it in the bushes beside the house. Then, a little at a time while pretending to be inspecting the few flowers the previous owners had planted that I hadn't managed to kill, we filled the cart and piled the remaining groceries by the kitchen door.

Then we cleared out the pantry and added the contents to the pile beside the door. Then we waited for sunset. We napped, but I couldn't sleep. Tate, on the other hand, dropped off almost immediately, so I spent the hours watching enviously and wishing I had his well-honed situational skills.

Eventually, the sun disappeared. There was a new moon so the night was dark, which was perfect for invisibility but would make travel difficult and slow. Tate woke as if by magic, fully and instantly as soon as true dark came and said, "It's time."

We gave Noble a tranquilizer so he'd not wake up, see that we were gone, and raise the alarm. While I waited for him to fall asleep, Tate sneaked out the back door and went along the trail he'd used when he checked out the spy. He'd made sure it was clear earlier, so he'd not step on any branches and give himself away.

We spoke mentally as he returned. *"He's still here and appears to be sleeping like a baby."*

"Don't believe it."

"I don't. I'm sure the second he hears an unexpected sound he'll be out of his car with an AK47."

As Tate's mental voice trailed off, I turned and there he was, in the Cape Cod mere inches away. "How'd you do that? I didn't hear you come in." Said out loud instead of mentally because we were together.

"Practice. You'd know how , too, if you'd lived the life I have."

Being together again felt right, especially knowing what we were about to do, and the dark added another dimension to my feelings. I wanted to say something but didn't know how to express myself.

"It's okay. I understand. We're in this together, and the smartest thing we can do is stick together like glue."

He understood and felt the same way. I wanted to lean into him to grab some of that know-how from his years of living a life so different from mine. He knew that too, and understood, and stepped close and wrapped his arms around me. I did lean into him, then, and wasn't embarrassed in the least.

We stayed that way for a good two minutes before, sighing, he pulled back and examined the outline of the two barely visible backpacks beside the kitchen door. "We should go."

We shouldered the backpacks and eased quietly out the back door. We moved slowly and quietly to the garden cart full of supplies. Tate grabbed the handle and we set off. We made good progress.

I offered to take my turn pulling the heavily laden cart but Tate insisted he could do it. Figuring he probably could do it best in the middle of the night in the middle of a forest, I subsided and didn't mention it again, but I wondered if his previous life had included sneaking between trees while pulling garden carts. Probably not.

When we reached my car, we unloaded the cart and returned for more supplies. This time we took turns. Tate didn't seem tired, but I couldn't imagine that he wasn't exhausted. I soon was.

We made two trips, one more than we'd expected, before pre-dawn crept through the trees. We had to almost run to get back to the Cape Cod before it grew light enough to be seen, but we made it, leaving the garden cart behind the bushes for still more trips the following night.

When I crawled into bed I had no problem falling asleep. Later, when I finally awoke, I was glad I'd filled Noble's food and water dishes because when I checked them, they were empty and my trusty companion was nowhere to be found. He'd gone about his day without waking me.

It was still light when I arose, late afternoon by my new burner phone. I checked Tate's room, opening his door softly. He was dead to the world so I closed it just as softly. Then I dressed and went outside, looking for Noble while making sure our spy saw me. Hopefully he'd not think anything of the fact that the first time I came outside was late in the afternoon.

Noble bounded over and I played with him in the yard until the sun touched the treetops and gave me an excuse to go back inside, making sure Noble came too. I locked the doggie door once he was inside, as I'd done the previous night. Then I drugged him. No sense taking chances on his waking up and going to look for us. I felt guilty but I did it.

Tate was up and looking as if he'd not spent the previous night pulling a large cart filled to the brim with heavy boxes and cans. He nodded to me shortly.

"Ready for another go at sneaking through the woods?"

"Yep." Our looks met in silent agreement that this was the right thing to do. The best way to stay alive and safe. "Tonight we bring clothes and personal stuff. It should be lighter."

"Whatever." Tate shrugged off the weight as if it was nothing and paced back and forth in his eagerness to get moving.

Was this love of danger a guy thing? I thought of my female friends and knew any number who'd be just as quick to dive into something exciting even if it could get them killed. Not me, I decided. I wasn't the type. But honesty compelled me to admit that if Tate wasn't in my life, my dislike of adventure could very well have landed me in some dungeon where I'd be experimented on by some psychotic scientist. Or worse.

"What are you thinking?" He stopped pacing. "Is there a problem?"

I colored. "No problem. Just considering the logistics involved in transferring enough stuff to supply us for an undetermined time without anyone knowing what we're doing."

He smiled. Rubbed his hands. Generally acted like the alpha male in his element. Danger. "It was my idea and it's working as I'd hoped. But I promise to do the heavy lifting."

I let him know what I thought about that and then we realized it was dark enough to get started. Noble's eyes were closing from the sedative and he was curled in his spot between the kitchen and living room.

We each shouldered a backpack, as we'd done the previous night, and headed for the garden cart that had been loaded after supper while we pretended once more to admire the previous owner's garden just in case our spy was close enough to see in the gathering dark. Tate grabbed the handle and we set off for a second night of traveling the forest road that we hoped the spy didn't know existed.

We made two trips that night, the same as the previous night, and when morning arrived the bulk of provisions had been transferred to my car. The little that remained was loaded into Tate's truck, a number of boxes and bags, and it was done in full sight of the spy. But Tate also made a conspicuous show of loading a tent and sleeping bag in the back in hopes the spy would buy the show we'd soon put on for his benefit.

I was groggy from lack of sleep. Tate was his usual alert self, but I saw weariness in his eyes and the drain on his body from the last two nights. I knew he was tired though he tried to pretend otherwise.

"Don't try to con me, Tate Brewster. I know how tired you are."

He gave up pretending. "Okay." He sighed. "I admit I'm tired, but I know my limit and I haven't come close to reaching it."

He was near enough that I could feel his breath. He took my face in his hands and silently asked me to look into his eyes and see the truth of his words and, yes, he was still capable of doing more than anyone I'd ever known. "Besides, once I'm in town I'll sleep in the truck while I wait for you." As his hands dropped, he added, "So I'll be fine."

I had no doubt he'd be okay. I wasn't so sure about myself, and Tate, too, had doubts. "You have your Glock. Keep it close and use it if necessary. Make sure it's in your pocket tonight when you leave, and is loaded, and be ready to grab it at the first hint of danger."

I promised with a voice that threatened to crack. Then we proceeded with the little show we'd carefully planned for the spy we knew was still positioned just out of sight because we kept careful track of his every move and every change of position.

He was currently behind a grove of trees where he was hidden from view, but he could still see the half of the driveway closest to the road. So our theatrical production was planned for that half.

Tate took the handful of doggie treats I gave him and went close to Noble so the dog would know what was in his hands. He gave Noble one treat and the greedy dog jumped on him, hoping for more. But, as planned, Tate held his hand back until Noble finally gave up and sulked in a corner of the kitchen to let Tate know how what he thought of being denied his rightful treats.

Then Tate grabbed a couple fishing rods I occasionally used, and I picked up my tackle box, and we headed for his truck that was conveniently parked far enough away from the Cape Cod that our spy could easily see it.

CHAPTER 13

Tate put the rods and tackle box in the back of the truck alongside the sleeping bag and tent. Then he turned to me. Gathered me in a romantic hug. Kissed me long and hard. Long enough and hard enough that I wished it wasn't an act. I felt his arousal and knew he felt my reaction. But we were putting on a play for an audience of one so we pulled apart so we could get on with the next act.

"I'll miss you." He sounded genuine and spoke loudly enough for the watcher to hear as he stared into my eyes. I was impressed with his acting ability.

"But the crappies are biting and I know how much you want to get a mess of them for dinner." I'd heard the fishermen in town talking, so that information was genuine. "And I like crappies too, so you'd better bring me enough to make up for being gone overnight." Also true if he was actually going to do some fishing. But he wasn't.

"I'll be back tomorrow if I don't catch anything," he said in the perfect imitation of a man who loved to fish. "But I'll be back the day after for sure."

"Promise?" I looked hard at him, and he winced like a man about to do a something his significant other might not like.

"I promise." He climbed into the truck and started the engine. But as he did, without being seen by the spy, he opened his hand so Noble could see the doggie treats and Noble, being the foodie he was, went running.

He jumped all over Tate in his eagerness for a treat and prevented him from closing the truck door. I could have hugged Noble for doing his part perfectly even though he didn't know he was acting. Tate looked over Noble at me and said, loudly enough for the spy to hear, "He wants to come."

I sighed as loudly as I could. "Okay. He saw the fishing poles and knows where you are going." Tate and I stared at each other long enough to make our watcher think we were debating what to do about the dog. Then I said, "Take him with you."

So Noble climbed into the truck with Tate and Tate drove off. Once on the highway, however, instead of going to a lake, he'd head to town where he and Noble would wait for me, and Tate could take the nap he so badly needed.

I went back into what was now a strangely empty Cape Cod and tried to sleep. I failed completely. Not only was the man I'd grown used to having around gone, but my companion of the last few years was also gone. Not to mention that someone with binoculars was spying on me and that someone had a rifle and undoubtedly knew how to use it. Yes, I had my Glock and had done a little shooting at the local range but that was all. Not enough for it to be a fair fight if I was forced to use it.

At least I didn't have to worry about Noble. No concern about him barking in the middle of the night or deciding to go in search of whatever animals prowled the dark because he'd be safely in the truck with Tate and they'd both be waiting for me in town. And, yes, if he wasn't with Tate, he'd be outside in the middle of the night. Because that's where I'd be.

I went outside and fussed with the yard, something I didn't normally do that would prove to the watcher that I was home. Then I quit because one look at my disreputable yard shouted that yard work wasn't my usual activity.

So I adjourned to the enclosed porch, where I spent the rest of the day working on art projects to sell to tourists. I'd never complete them because I'd be gone. Forever? The question haunted me and the resulting works would never sell because they were terrible, but the effort kept me busy and was definitely usual for me, not to mention that it kept my mind off the coming night as much as anything could.

Midafternoon I tried to nap. I failed, of course, just as I'd failed to sleep before. But I rested and watched the sun track across the bedroom ceiling as I wondered if I'd ever be in that room again. When the sun had dipped low enough that it no longer shone through the window, I turned onto my side, closed my eyes tight, and willed myself to sleep.

An unknown number of hours later, I awoke to a night not quite as dark as the first night because it was no longer a new moon, but it was dark enough to hide me and definitely dark enough to make walking treacherous.

I rose, dressed in dark clothes, took the Glock from the drawer beside my bed and shoved it into a pocket of the black hoodie I donned, and headed for the kitchen door. On impulse, I took a tiny flashlight from a kitchen drawer and stuck it in another pocket of the hoodie. I wouldn't use it until I was safely past any possibility of being seen, but I liked the feel of it in one pocket as much as I liked the feel of the Glock in another.

Though it wasn't as dark as during my previous trips, I was now alone, and that made this night worse. Darker. Scarier. I'd never been a coward, never been afraid of the unknown, never hesitated to do anything in the dark that I'd do during the day. But if things went wrong, I'd have no help, and I was terrified.

I crept slowly and silently to the forest road. Once there I paused and took stock of my surroundings, choosing the exact middle of the road because I could see that. I didn't want to chance running into a bush on either side that might alert the watcher to my presence. And I set off.

It went well but slowly. I had no way of telling time and the minutes dragged. I stopped often, not to rest because I was too hyper to be tired, rather to make sure nothing was wrong. I turned completely around every time I stopped, and I checked every shadow, but everything was as it should be.

For a while.

Somehow, I strayed from the center of the road to one side and tripped over a tree root. I fell onto a bush and made enough noise to wake the dead. Guilt and fear washed over me as I heard a car door opening from the direction of the spy. Soon I heard someone crashing through the trees in my direction and saw the beam of a powerful flashlight moving back and forth and coming closer. And closer.

I pulled my hoodie further over my head and rolled

face down in the dirt and prayed not to be spotted. I went as silent as possible and prayed the flashlight beam wouldn't reach me and, if it did, that my black clothing would blend in with the ground and the surrounding brush.

The watcher came straight towards me. He clearly was experienced in moving through a forest because he didn't let trees or brush confuse him. He knew where the sound had come from, and he zeroed in on that spot. On me.

I waited to be found.

Then a miracle happened. His thrashing had startled a deer that had been grazing not far away. The flashlight's beam caught the deer and scared it even more. It rose on its hind legs, then bolted, crashing through the trees, and making even more noise than I'd made when I fell.

"Stupid deer." The watcher turned and stomped back to his vehicle. I heard the slam of its door as he returned to his perch. And I silently thanked the deer for saving me, though I waited for a long time before moving even enough to roll over and see the starlit sky.

I got up in increments. After I sat up, I waited a good half hour by my calculations before moving to a kneeling position, and then another half hour before standing. Still more time passed before I carefully returned to the center of the forest road, holding my breath that I'd not step on any twigs and bring the watcher back.

I used the tiny flashlight to make sure I was where I wanted to be, bending close to the ground and shielding its beam with my hand. Then I waited, but no sound came from the watcher.

I carefully resumed my trek, but at least an hour had been lost, possibly more, and I hadn't noted the time when I left the Cape Cod and didn't know how long I'd slept. Would I reach my car before dawn? I didn't dare move faster because that could bring more unwanted attention. All I could do was pray the sun would stay away until I was safe.

My mouth was in my throat as the dark lessened and I could begin to make out the edges of the forest road. But that meant I could move faster, so I sped up as much as I dared as colors slowly appeared. Morning birds came out and sang loudly. I was sure they were reminding me that I still had a long trek.

I finally speeded to a trot, reasoning that I was far enough past the watcher that he'd not hear, but I kept a close watch on the ground ahead for obstructions now that the rising sun put everything in clear relief.

It was full daylight when I reached the end of my journey. I was tempted to make a mad dash to the car and peel out of there in record time. Instead, as we'd agreed when we'd formed a plan, I hid behind a thicket and then moved through it slowly and carefully enough not to make a sound. I visually checked the car. It was still locked and, therefore, empty except for the provisions stacked in the back seat and in the trunk. And no sights or sounds from wildlife said anyone else was there.

I pulled the car keys from my back pocket and let my finger hover over the 'open' function so the doors would unlock when I was close and I'd be able to climb in quickly. I didn't unlock them sooner because the beep would be a dead giveaway if anyone was listening.

I didn't dare start the engine remotely for the same

reason. Finally, when I couldn't think of another thing to do to assure my safe passage, I took a deep breath and ran as fast as I knew how, pressing 'unlock' as I ran. The doors were unlocked by the time I reached it and it started at the first turn of the key. Most importantly, no one came at me.

I pulled onto the road. I'd have to pass the watcher. There was no help for it because it was a dead-end road, but he didn't know my car so shouldn't react when I went by. I'd go at a normal speed. Nothing to arouse his suspicion. It might work. I prayed it would. I pulled the hoodie over my head and held the steering wheel tight as I approached his car pulled to the side of the road. Then I was beside him.

And safely past. I was about to give a sigh of relief when I glanced in the rear-view mirror. What I saw made my hands grip the steering wheel tighter.

He'd not paid any attention as I approached, nor as I passed. But once I was far enough past for him to see my license plate, he'd looked through a pair of binoculars and read the plate number. Then he pulled out a paper and checked it. Looked again at the license plate. And started his car.

He had my license plate number and knew who I was. I had to get out of there. Fast.

CHAPTER 14

I stepped on the gas and the car jumped ahead, as the watcher pulled onto the road and accelerated. But I had a head start. It had taken time to check the license plate. I had a chance. But I was an average driver. I had to assume he was an expert.

I reached the main road. Which way to go? To town where Tate might be able to help? But town was miles away and on a straight road that allowed for speed. I'd not make it judging from the speed of the car behind me, accelerating with each second as if the driver was a professional.

If I went in the opposite direction, there were a number of small roads branching off from the main road, and the main road itself curved around lakes and ponds and over numerous hills. There were many places where I'd not be seen momentarily by someone chasing me, though I'd be going away from town and the safety of a public place.

I turned away from town and went as fast as I dared. I approached a curve and went around it without slowing down. I lost the watcher, but he'd only be out of sight for seconds.

I looked ahead. More curves. More hills. And a

logging road I knew of that was only visible to someone who knew the area. Was my pursuer local? Did he know about it? I decided to take the chance and wheeled onto the logging road and then whipped behind a dense thicket just as my pursuer appeared. I held my breath and waited.

He barreled past, still accelerating, and was soon out of sight. How long would it take him to realize he'd lost me? Minutes? Seconds? I had to hurry. I pulled back onto the road and turned towards town, going as fast as I dared.

I turned off of it and onto the second side road I came across. Not the first because he might expect me to take it, so I passed that one and took the second. Then, when I reached another intersection, I turned again. And at the next crossing I turned still again. I continued my zig zag path until I reached town. It took much longer than it should have, but I didn't see anyone behind me as I pulled into a back, shady street with a few houses straggling along it.

"I was followed."

"Are you safe?"

"I think so. I'll be there in seconds."

"Don't come here. It's in the open. Park behind the grain elevator. It's the biggest building in town and the least likely place he'll look for you. I'll meet you there."

I pulled behind the elevator as Tate arrived, Noble sticking his head out the window looking for me. I jumped out and ran to open the truck door and hugged him as Tate said, "We have to assume we don't have much time so we should hurry."

"What about the bank?"

"We need cash so we take a chance and hope he won't think to look there."

We locked Noble in the truck with a partially open window and enough treats to keep him happy. The previous day we'd picked up the necessary paperwork for the bank, me to close out my account and Tate to withdraw as much as was currently in his account in his home bank. He'd set up things so he could withdraw amounts no matter where he was. "Hopefully the banks have implemented communication so we won't have to wait."

We separated when we went inside. We agreed on a meeting place about a mile out of town on a road near the beginning of a trail, a grassy area where hikers parked their cars. It was remote and not well maintained so there was a lot of undergrowth.

I'd park behind bushes and hope they were thick. When Tate arrived, he wouldn't get out. Instead, I'd simply follow his truck and we'd disappear. That's what would happen if everything went according to plan.

The bank was busy. I waited in line forever before being led to a desk and a young, smiling woman who looked like a teenager and was probably older than me. "You want to close out your account?" I said I did. "Is there a problem?" I said there was no problem. "I hope you've been satisfied with our service." I said I'd been more than happy but I was in a hurry. How to say so without arousing suspicion?

I looked at the wall clock. "Is it that late?" I made myself look surprised. Concerned. "Oh dear."

Wrong thing to say. "If you're in a hurry maybe you should come back some other day." She smiled a smile of white, flossed teeth. "We don't want to rush anything and get it wrong."

"I have the paperwork all filled out and I do need to get on the road, and I need to go today. I've got a reservation, you see, and I'd like to get there before dark."

Would she buy it? The smile was replaced by a look of slight annoyance, but she took my paperwork and scanned it quickly. "This shouldn't take long." She read the details. "You haven't lived here long compared to some of the people who bank here."

I tried to sit still but wiggled in impatience. She noticed and the slight frown deepened. "We'll see about taking care of this in a timely manner." Her voice left no doubt that she disapproved of hurrying even the least little bit.

"Tate, don't wait until I'm done. At the rate this woman is working, it'll be closing time before I get out of here."

His voice came back. *"Mine won't take long. It never does. It's a simple transfer of funds. See if you can hurry her up."*

I tried but the harder I tried the slower she worked. I glanced out the large window at the front of the bank and almost puked. A black car with the Weather For America logo was cruising the main street. From one end to the other and then back again. Slowly.

"He's here."

"He's just checking. He doesn't know for sure that we're here, and the grain elevator isn't likely on his list of places we might be found."

The bank president came out of his office. I looked his way and the teller handling my account followed my gaze. It was clear that she wondered if I knew the president and decided it might be in her best interests to make me happy, just in case he and I were friends. And she finally started the process of closing out my account and handing me a surprisingly large amount of money.

"It's a rather lot of cash to be carrying. Are you sure you don't want me to transfer it somewhere?"

I took the cash. It would pay our way longer than I'd expected. Since moving into the Cape Cod, I'd been so afraid of running out of money that I'd been overly cautious about financial outlays. Now I realized that I could have hired a carpenter to fix the many problems in my house, but I was glad I'd not known how comfortable I was because the bulge in my purse was reassuring. "Yes, I'm sure. Don't worry, it'll be tucked safely away very soon."

She gave me another sparkling smile to tell me our business was concluded, and then smiled even brighter as the bank president walked past. As I rose and headed for the back door of the bank, I decided she'd go far in the banking business.

Tate finished at the same time and we met at the door. We stepped through and gauged the distance from the back of the bank to the back of the grain elevator. It would be a long walk behind several buildings, but they were close enough to each other that if we crossed the spaces between them quickly, we were unlikely to be spotted.

"Come on." Tate grabbed my hand and we moved out and reached the car and truck without any problem. "Follow me." He climbed into the truck, and soon we were cautiously nosing out from behind the grain elevator and onto the main street because there was no way to reach the highway except by going across it.

"He's at the far end of the street. He's not turning yet. He's not looking this way."

"Go now!" The truck entered the main street and I followed. We drove as fast as we dared.

We almost made it. Tate's truck turned off the main street and onto the highway access. I followed, but before I'd gone the distance and reached the highway, the black car turned, and the driver saw me.

He sped up but dared not go so fast that people would call the authorities. We, on the other hand, were on the highway and could go at highway speeds. *"We need to lose him. Is there a way we can get lost?"*

The highway was a straight path through curvy gravel roads that went over the hills and around the lakes that had enabled me to lose the watcher earlier. There were few off-ramps leading to those roads, but there was also a turn-around just ahead, and beyond it was an off-ramp that led to a sprinkling of cottages and resorts threaded in a haphazard manner among the many lakes of the area. The place was a maze to anyone who didn't know the area. I hoped our follower didn't. I said to Tate, *"Take the U- turn, and then take the first off-ramp."*

The truck was already so close to the turn-around that it careened around it on two wheels. But it settled back down and soon Tate and I were off the highway and seeking shelter among the trees that grow thickly beside lakes. We found a locked gate leading to a summer home that wasn't occupied at the moment. Tate broke the lock and opened the gate and we drove through and around a curve in the driveway. Then he replaced the lock and the gate. Then we waited to see if we'd been followed.

Tate got out of the truck, and I joined him. Noble was insulted that he couldn't run around a place so full of squirrels, but he only had a cracked window to provide fresh air, and I hoped he'd not start barking. Or that, if he did, that anyone listening would hear just another annoyingly noisy dog.

We waited three hours. Then we walked out to the road. Tate went one way, staying to the side and darting from one tree to the next while I did the same the other way. Neither of us saw the WFA car, and we returned to Noble and our hiding place hoping we'd lost him. "Now we wait for dark, and do what we can to make the vehicles untraceable."

We mixed dirt with bottled water because it was the only water we had. There was a lake beyond the house, but we didn't dare cross the yard to reach it because the area wasn't isolated. We smeared the resulting mud over enough of the license plates to make them unreadable and then more on the tailgates so it would appear the mud was from driving through mud puddles.

We made sandwiches from our abundant supplies and made Noble happy with the left-overs. We hoped the owners of the lake house wouldn't choose that moment to visit their summer place, and they didn't, though we heard the sounds of activity in the houses on either side. Fortunately the greenery was thick enough that no one spotted us.

We kept quiet, and I gave Noble half of a tranquilizer. It was the last one. Now I had only half a pill should we need to keep him silent again.

I wouldn't leave him behind. Not Noble. I told Tate

as much, and he agreed. Noble was one of us, and we'd keep him with us no matter what. Then we settled down in our respective vehicles, and waited for dark.

CHAPTER 15

We moved out as soon as the sun went down. We didn't wait for full dark because we wanted to put on as many miles as possible and we figured the muddy plates would be unreadable in the dimness of evening. But I was tired. I'd not slept since leaving the Cape Cod. Tate had napped in town waiting for me, but he was probably tired too.

I didn't know how many hours we drove with me following Tate. I only knew the time came that I had to mentally contact him. *"I can't go much farther. I need sleep."*

"We've gone a long way. It should be safe to stop. I'll look for a motel with a back parking lot. I'll ask for a back room."

"Will they be suspicious?"

"A little more money will help if that happens. I'll say we eloped and are afraid your family is looking for us. I'll say they don't like me."

The motel clerk was suspicious of two vehicles in the middle of the night who wanted to pay cash. So Tate gave him the full phony love story. The clerk said there was no such thing as true love, and if we actually were eloping then we were as dumb as a box of rocks.

A few bills made him change his mind about

sending us on into the night, and a few more allowed Noble to stay in a motel that didn't allow pets. As he scooped the bills into his pocket he said he enjoyed helping two lovers start a new life together. As Tate relayed it to me later, the whole thing sounded rather sickening, but by that time I was so tired I hardly heard his explanation as he carried the backpacks containing clothes and our personal things into the honeymoon suite, which was the only back room available. It was all I could do to wake Noble long enough to get him inside too.

Being the honeymoon suite, there was only one bed with a padded heart-shaped headboard. I was too tired to shudder at the sight. I just fell onto it, and Tate had to roll me to one side so he could pull down the covers. Then he undressed me enough to be comfortable but not enough to be indecent, shoved me back to the side of the bed I'd dropped onto, and pulled the covers over me.

I supposed he slept too. Next to me. I didn't know and didn't care. I barely managed to stay awake long enough to hear Noble's nails clicking on the floor to know he was with us. As soon as I heard him curl up at the foot of the bed, I forgot the world.

In the morning Tate was, as usual, bright, cheerful, and fully awake. I knew because the door flying open jolted me awake. He entered with two coffees and a couple rolls, compliments of the motel, and a smile broad enough to make even grumpy me happy. "Are you awake?"

I pulled the covers over my head and closed my eyes against the bright sun streaming through the door behind and around him, only noticing in some small part of my brain that had managed to come awake that he was one awesome male.

But the smell of coffee and rolls prevented me from falling back to sleep. We'd not eaten since leaving the deserted driveway, and knowing food was close made my stomach rumble. The rolls smelled like they were to die for, probably homemade by the owner's wife. It was, after all, a remote mom and pop motel in the middle of somewhere.

"Where are we?" I struggled up and stared with distaste at my dirty self and longingly at the bathroom. The steamy mirror said Tate had already used the shower. "Will the coffee stay hot while I clean up?"

"I doubt it, but I can get more." He kicked the door shut and set the breakfast stuff on the tiny table beneath the TV. "And to answer your next question, we are in the middle of nowhere, and as far as I can tell no one checked in after us, and this is the only motel in the area, so I think we weren't followed."

He took a drag of his coffee and swallowed one of the rolls in a single bite. "When you are awake, there's something we need to discuss." The look he gave me that went from top to bottom and back again said he doubted that would happen soon.

But he didn't know me. When I emerged, clean and in fresh clothes, to enjoy the new coffee and more rolls because he'd eaten mine, I was as awake as he was. After giving me an approving look, he smoothed the bed covers so we could sit facing each other as he began. "We should ditch our vehicles."

I almost choked on my awesome cinnamon roll. "Why?"

"Because any respectable spy would have placed

tracking devices on them."

He was right. "Your truck, yes. I can see that. But they haven't seen my car except after it was too late to do anything."

"They had your license plate number. They could easily have asked around town and found it in the repair shop. It would only take a few seconds to stick an air tag on it."

"We can look for the tag."

"There are so many places a device can be put on a vehicle that we can't hope to find every single one without tearing it apart, and we don't have the time. Besides, if we do look and we find one, we can't know if it's the only one, or if it was intentionally put somewhere easy to find so we'd stop looking for the second one they put somewhere that's harder to find. And then a third. And so on."

He cleared his throat. "Which was why I insisted we bring the titles with us." At the time he'd not said why, and I'd thought it was in case I never returned to the Cape Cod.

I finished my coffee and roll in silence and dropped the cup in the wastebasket. "Okay." What else could I say? "How do we do that?"

"We find a small, local used car dealership, and tell the salesman we want to trade. And we pay cash."

I breathed deeply. "Yesterday I thought we had a lot of cash. Now it feels like a pitiful amount."

"Once we stop running, we won't spend much."

"There's a lot of stuff to transfer to different cars."

"We'll work fast." I sighed, thinking how helpful Noble wouldn't be. With my dog's help we'd get the job done, but not as quickly as Tate expected.

We found a small used car lot in the second town. We'd have missed it if not for a farm truck we couldn't get around that moved so slowly we saw everything around us. Correction, I saw it because of the farm truck. Tate saw it because he was Tate. We wheeled into the lot as the farm truck crept away.

"These will do nicely." Tate chose two Ford Ranger trucks. "Not too big, not too small, and they won't attract attention. One was dark blue, the other medium brown. I'd miss my cute, red car, but I wouldn't miss being chased.

The salesman, who was most likely also the owner, didn't blink at our wanting to trade as he looked over our trade-ins. "One old truck that'd due for the scrap heap, and one tiny car that no one in the country will want." Forget that Tate's truck was a classic and mine was shiny and clean. "I can see why you guys want decent transportation that'll carry things." His eyebrows rose at the boxes and bags we were carrying. "Where are you headed with all that stuff? To the moon?"

Tate laughed and didn't answer. The salesman eyed our cash and checked the titles to make sure they weren't counterfeit. Once he determined they were legitimate, his eyes lit up and he upped the price. He'd smile all the way to the bank, but the trucks were perfect for our purpose, so we made the deal. He helped us move boxes and cheerfully waved us on our way as we left.

As we had breakfast in the next town's café, Tate said it would take a while for the titles to clear. "By the time WFA knows they're chasing the wrong vehicles, we'll be safe."

"Which will be where, exactly?"

"You'll see. A good place, but we won't take a direct route. Just in case."

"And you know how to throw off anyone following us?"

He grinned broadly. "Of course I do." He hated the danger we were in, but loved the cat and mouse game he was playing with our pursuers. I shuddered, slathered a piece of toast with jam, and ignored the grin.

We drove for two more days, staying in mom and pop motels and paying in cash. Each time Tate explained that we were moving to explain the trucks loaded with boxes, and we shared a room. And a bed because a married couple asking for separate rooms might raise red flags, but those nights I wasn't so exhausted that he had to put me to bed like a child. I could do that myself. And did. And we slept well.

But during the nights, when I'd awaken, I'd be totally aware of the sleeping man beside me, and I both felt the pull of his male body and the mystery of him. The things I knew about him, as well as those things I didn't know.

The second morning, as we ate our complimentary breakfast in our room instead of in their breakfast room to avoid the possibility of someone remembering us afterwards, I asked him about himself.

He shrugged and brushed crumbs away. "Not much to tell. The usual military story."

"No family? No girlfriend?"

Another shrug. "Some guys could handle a family and the kind of life we lived. I figured it was easier not to even try, and it worked for me." He eyed me carefully, one part at a time. "I'm done with that life."

"Instead, you are running from people who want to

do unspeakable things to you."

"And to do similar things you." He dropped the paper plate and cup in the wastebasket. "This life is different." His eyes lit up as if hiding in a motel room was a positive experience. "No one telling me when to get up, when to go to sleep, and what to do in between." His eyes positively glowed. "I like that."

Which meant he truly believed we had a future. The thought was encouraging enough that I finished my own breakfast, dropped my trash in the wastebasket, and followed him into the bright day without fearing what the coming hours would bring.

When the day ended without any indication of our being followed, I decided our invisibility was only to be expected given how knowledgeable we were about such things. Okay, how knowledgeable Tate was. But I was with him and learning something new every day. Given enough time, I'd be a pretty good spy.

That didn't happen because after two days of circuitous driving until I couldn't have said where we were and could only know the direction by tracking the sun's path across the sky, I followed him when he turned into what looked like bare forest but was actually a twisted, bumpy path that could only be traversed by four-wheel drive vehicles. My little red car wouldn't have survived.

It meandered through wilderness so dense that we had to stop several times to pull large tree limbs aside in order to continue. After we passed, we put them back. Since we left no tire tracks in the rocky terrain, no one could know we'd been there.

Then we arrived. I sat for a while staring at the place that would be our home for the foreseeable future, and even Tate didn't get out immediately. I wondered what he thought of the cabin in front of us. If he'd been there before. If he knew what it would be like.

It was a small log cabin, small as in having two rooms at the most. Probably just one. There was an outhouse to the back on one side. Solar panels on the roof hinted at electric power, and a propane tank could be for cooking, so that was something.

Mostly, though, I noted that it was isolated even more than the Cape Cod, at the end of an impassable path that in no way could be construed as being an actual road and was hidden by the towering evergreens we'd traveled through for the past few hours, and its size made it even less noticeable. In one way it was awful. In another, more important way, it was perfect.

CHAPTER 16

I followed Tate inside, each of us carrying the first of the many boxes we'd recently transferred to the trucks as Noble supervised with a helpful wag of his tail. Once inside we looked around, and I breathed a sigh of relief. "It's livable. I was concerned after seeing the outside."

Tate nodded, checking out the large main room with a small room in one corner. "An indoor bathroom. A plus. The outhouse must be for decoration. Or is left over from before Billy bought the place."

I did my own inspection. "He must have done considerable remodeling because the inside is quite nice." It was clean and modern with stairs leading to a sleeping loft. The only dust was the inevitable layer from not being occupied. A modern kitchen promised that the bathroom would also be decent. The whole place looked comfortable and convenient with a couch and chairs scattered about and a huge table in the center. There was a desk against one wall.

"It's a great get-away, and it looks like it was designed for one person."

"Billy's a bachelor." Tate gave me a look I

couldn't interpret. "We'll manage. We've managed so far."

"We had no choice. We were chased by an unhinged maniac."

"That won't be a problem while we're here, and we can stay as long as we choose."

We checked the loft and discovered five single beds along the back wall "Looks like a military barracks."

"Billy was in the Army."

"Why five beds for one person?"

"He said he wants to bring his buddies and go hunting." He looked through the only window visible from the loft to a nearby stream that fell in a white, foamy rush to the bottom of the hill that held the cabin. "And fishing."

There were fishing poles on the walls and a locked gun safe in one corner. "No buddies here at the moment so we have a choice of beds." Tate's raised eyebrow said he'd let me choose first and expected I'd take the farthest one. He'd be a gentleman and take the one on the opposite side.

I wanted to get a meal started before anything else. "I'm tired of eating in cafes. I want real food."

Tate thought Billy might have food somewhere since the whole place was not only comfortable, it was well organized. "It's ready to be lived in at a moment's notice." Sure enough, we found a trap door that led to a full, finished, basement with a very large freezer stocked with all kinds of meat and fish, along with a small assortment of vegetables. "Billy's an accomplished hunter and fisherman, but he buys his vegetables at the store, and he's definitely a meat eater instead of a vegetarian."

"I'll start a garden." Tate's expression said he'd noticed the lack of a garden at the Cape Cod. He dropped the freezer door shut after I selected a nice roast and a package of frozen vegetables as I said, "If we leave, then this Billy person, whoever he is, can harvest what I sow."

"Unless we're still here."

"That would mean your friend would give up his cabin for a long time. That would be asking a lot."

"Billy would do it. We go way back."

"It's still a lot, even for a good friend."

"He's a nice guy. Sociable. The kind of guy who knows everyone and likes them, and if there's someone he doesn't know, then he knows someone who does know that person."

"We could use someone like that."

"Yes we could, which is why I thought of him as soon as I knew we were being watched." Tate turned to bring in another box from the truck. "I knew we were in deep and might need his special kind of help." I followed to do the same. "Which is why I asked him to meet us here as soon as he can get a leave of absence."

He pulled a box from the back of his pickup and shouldered it. "Though it'll be a while since it hasn't been that long since his last one." He carried the box up the stairs and into the cabin that already felt like home, as I carried another and looked around to decide what to do with all the things we'd brought. It wasn't a large cabin and the basement was full.

"How will he know we've arrived?"

Tate flexed his shoulders before heading back outside for the next box. And the next. "No cell service, but he knew we were headed here. He'll come when he can. In the meantime, we settle in and enjoy the wilderness life."

I thought about the guns and fishing rods so prominently displayed in the loft. "Do you fish or hunt?"

"Some. I suspect I'll get a lot of practice while I'm here. How's Noble as a hunting dog?"

"Squirrels, maybe, so don't expect much." Noble moved close to Tate with a haughty expression that said he was an expert hunter and how dare I say otherwise, as I wondered if we'd be there long enough for living off the land to become a part of our routine.

When the trucks were empty, we parked them in a shed that passed for a garage. Tate approved. "Out of sight. We're the only ones who know they are there." There was space in the shed to hide several full sized vehicles. Was that intentional? Tate's friend seemed almost paranoid about privacy, a fact in our favor.

There was a fire ring in the yard. I looked forward to a campfire until Tate said, "No fire. Nothing to let anyone know the cabin is occupied."

"What about the wood burning stove?" It sat against one wall with chairs on either side. "Must we freeze if it turns cold?"

He pointed to a thermostat on the wall. "The stove is for enjoyment. It's a cabin and cabins have wood stoves, but the solar array Billy installed along with the propane provide all the power needed for a stove, heat, air conditioning, and everything else. It's quiet, efficient, and undetectable."

We had stew for dinner. I had no idea what kind of meat was in it. Something from a hunting expedition. It was wonderful after motel rolls and café meals. We pulled dark curtains across the windows before it got dark, making sure each window was fully covered. I noticed that the curtains were the blackout kind.

Tate was grateful for the thick curtains. He considered them just another precaution, like the lack of a campfire, and was glad Billy had thought to install them. Was it a necessary precaution? I didn't ask. I just pulled them tight and tucked my curiosity about the owner of the cabin in some region of my brain that was learning how people survived when they were on the run. I was learning fast.

Morning came, then morphed into afternoon and eventually into evening and another night in a routine that repeated each time the sun came up though we didn't know it because the windows were blacked out. I was glad for the clock on my burner phone.

The days blurred into one another until I forgot to count them. I should have marked them on the calendar on the kitchen wall but didn't think to do so when we arrived and didn't know what day it was when I realized I should have done so. Then I realized it didn't truly matter.

We were in a lovely cabin in a gorgeous and quite wild forest, and we had nothing pressing to do except exist and, as time passed, we learned quite well how to do that.

Tate fished and hunted. I cooked long, leisurely meals and checked the ground outside with an eye to a garden that I didn't dare plant because that would alert any watcher that the cabin was occupied.

Noble loved everything about our new existence. The squirrels that he never managed to catch. Hunting with Tate and retrieving game after Tate showed him where it was and what was expected of him. He watched Tate fish downstream where the creek widened and the white water turned into a surprisingly deep pond before continuing on to wherever it went.

The water was cold, something I learned after deciding to go for a swim. Watching from the shore Tate laughed as I climbed back out as soon as I jumped in, shivering and hopping about until the sun warmed me back to a more human temperature. But he, too, ended up in the water for a lovely, relaxing afternoon.

I grew to love the covered porch because, since we couldn't have a campfire, we spent the waning hours of the afternoon in the chairs we dragged there, and watched the sun go down before going in to close the curtains and spend the rest of the evening inside because once we turned on the lights we didn't venture outside lest a ray of light through an open door give us away.

Each day we lingered a little longer on the porch than the day before until the day came that we watched the world turn dark enough that the day birds went silent and the night birds started calling to each other.

And still we sat and let the night seep into us.

"Nice, isn't it?"

"Why the telepathy? No one is around to overhear us."

" I know, but silence just feels right. Anything said out loud would break the spell."

"I agree."

Tate scooted his chair closer to mine and took my hand. He didn't say anything out loud or mentally because words of any kind would jar the peace that pooled around us. We sat like that until it was so dark I couldn't make out his features, just the outline of his body next to mine. And still we sat until the moon rose and cast its pale light across the forest.

Then we saw something different. Another light that was neither pale nor from the sky. "Someone's coming."

We went inside but didn't turn on the lights. Tate locked the door and grabbed his rifle, while indicting that I get my Glock. I did but it was important to keep Noble quiet, so I stuck the Glock in my belt as Tate motioned for Noble and me to go up to the loft.

We did and went silent. Tate stood to one side of the door and slid off the safety as we heard footsteps on the porch.

Someone pounded on the door. "Hey in there! Tate old buddy, it's me. Billy. I came a long way because you asked me to, and this is my place so let me in. Okay?"

Even in the dark I could see Tate's form relaxing as he set the rifle aside and opened the door. "It's about time. I thought you'd never come."

The two men hugged as I put the Glock back beneath my pillow and gave Noble a hug so he'd know he'd been a good, quiet dog. The men below separated and pulled the blackout curtains tight even though they were already closed in an abundance of caution. When they were sure no light showed, they turned on the lights.

Then Noble and I went to the railing and showed ourselves. Tate looked up at us and his friend followed his glance. He waved lazily. "Hi. You must be Zoe. Tate told me about you."

He had the same military haircut Tate had had when we first met, and the same way of standing straight and proud that Tate would probably never change. He had the same way of looking around in a way that said he saw everything in a glance. After that, the resemblance ended.

CHAPTER 17

Billy was shorter than Tate, and rounder. I liked him instantly and was pretty sure most people had a similar reaction. What had Tate said? That his friend knew everyone, and everyone liked him? Of course they did because they instinctively recognized a genuinely nice guy. The proof was that he answered Tate's call for help, offered his home as a safe house, and was standing in the middle of the room asking what he could do for us.

Tate had said something else about his friend. That he could find out everything about anything given a bit of time to work on it. I could think of a million things I wanted to know.

But it was the middle of the night so they didn't settle in for a gossip session. Instead Billy dragged a duffle bag up the stairs and diplomatically chose the middle bed after checking which ones were available, and he didn't make a single snide remark about Tate and me sleeping on opposite ends of the loft. Instead, he plunked himself on his chosen bed and said it had been a long drive and he planned to sleep like a log. Then he undressed to his skivvies, rolled into bed, and was dead to the world.

In the morning Tate and I tiptoed around him. When we went downstairs, Tate moved Billy's SUV into the shed and brought the rest of his gear inside, consisting of what looked like a single bag of groceries. By then Billy was awake, I had breakfast started, and I expected we'd get acquainted. Billy had other ideas.

"Tell me all about this situation you two are in that you didn't explain over the phone," he said without preamble as he and Tate grabbed coffee and settled at the table in the middle of the cabin. "What trouble have you managed to get yourself into now, my friend?"

Tate explained. Billy listened without interrupting but his eyes grew wide and then wider still as the more outlandish aspects of our situation were made clear. "Telepathy? Really?"

"Something close if not actual telepathy. Mind to mind speech, no sound involved, and distance doesn't seem to make any difference."

Billy whistled. "Think of the implications. The military would love to get their hands on what you have. And about a million greedy civilian companies and more. Because it's huge. You'd have no peace."

"That's the problem."

"Who's after you? The government?" Tate explained about Weather For America. "What's their deal? Was it deliberate? Did they target you or was it an accident?"

I joined them at the table. "We don't know the answers to those questions. We just know they came after us as soon as they confirmed we'd been exposed to the wind, and they've followed us ever since. Or tried to."

Billy inspected Tate. "My friend here has certain

invaluable skills, and this place is as safe as anyplace on the planet. I made sure of that when I bought it." He reached for the bag of what I'd thought were groceries and pulled out several smaller, plastic bags. "Sat phones. A dozen of them, and I can get more if needed." He waved one through the air. "All untraceable and in no way connected to any of us."

He handed us each a phone. "Use them sparingly, and do not ever call friends or family. Only me. And just because I bought them anonymously doesn't mean nasty people can't trace them given enough time."

He continued like a teacher lecturing a class. "Every so often toss your current one in the trash after having smashed it to bits and soaked it in water overnight, and then replace it with a new one." He got one for himself. "I'll do the same." Tate nodded as if this was standard procedure. "They were purchased at different places at different times and always with cash."

"Thanks," was Tate's simple reply. I merely stared at my new phone in a kind of dazed wonder.

Billy filled a plate with hash and refilled his coffee. "I'll head out tomorrow and see what I can find out about WFA."

"I'll come with you." Tate topped his hash with a couple eggs.

Billy held up a hand. "No. They are looking for you. You stay here."

Tate didn't like that. "It's my problem, not yours. The phones are untraceable and we're hundreds of miles from where it happened and thousands of miles away from any normal WFA installation."

"And all that doesn't mean a thing." Billy refilled

his plate, gave me a nod to say it was good, and continued. "I don't plan to use these phones. Instead, I'll buy a new one, use it in the nearest café, and then dump it in the trash after smashing it to pieces."

The more they talked the more my stomach roiled to the point that I couldn't eat though something went through me – some sensation – that felt what they planned was right for the situation. "What can you find out that we don't already know?" No more fishing for Tate and cooking for me and both of us watching sunsets turn into night. I didn't know how I knew those things were in the past, but I did. I knew.

Tate spoke. "When Billy returns, he'll know everything there is to know about Weather For America, and more." Tate had no doubt about his friend's special skill.

"If you're going to do all that over a sat phone, why go away? Why not call from here?"

Billy shoved his breakfast aside. "Little girl, let me tell you something about life. Three facts, and the first fact is that you should never believe anything anyone says. Ever. Not even me. Which means that just because I said you are safe here doesn't mean you are. It only means I think it is.

" Fact number two is that making calls from some place far away using a phone that can't be traced and dumping it immediately won't necessarily keep me safe. Or you.

"Fact number three expands on fact number two. If I make said calls in the morning, leave as soon as I dump the phone and then drive in random directions until dark, I might still be followed because absolutely nothing anyone can do guarantees anything. Ever."

Tate nodded agreement. I gulped and cleared the table as I tucked Billy's words into the back of my mind to think about later. Then I scraped left-over breakfast into Noble's dish and watched the two men head outside for what turned out to be the kind of guy reunion that hadn't happened the night before.

How could they laugh and slap each other on the back after Billy's scary little speech? I decided I didn't understand guys. Some guys, anyway. Guys like Tate and Billy. The uber male, uber confident military type. I found Noble, stuck some doggie treats in my pocket, and the two of us went for a walk because he was the kind of male animal I understood.

The next morning Billy left and Tate began pacing. "I should have gone too."

"He thought you should stay here."

"He might not know the right questions to ask, or when to press for more information."

"What's his track record like?"

Tate stopped. Flushed. "Close to perfect."

I went close. "Then trust him." But his mind was elsewhere. He couldn't stay still. He needed to work off restless energy. "Noble and I went for a walk earlier. I saw some stuff that could make lovely collages, but I didn't have anything to carry them in." I moved closer still until I could feel his breath and the warmth radiating from his body. The excess energy that needed to be worked off somehow. "Will you come and help carry some stuff?"

He stopped mid-step and slanted a look at me that said he knew exactly what I was trying to do and that he appreciated it. "Yes I will, and I'm sorry for acting like an immature idiot."

"You? Immature? An idiot?" The idea was so ludicrous that I laughed out loud. Noble came to see what the commotion was about, and soon the three of us were foraging among hundred foot tall pine trees for odd items that could be turned into what I thought of as tourist art. Nothing I could use until I was home, but when we returned from the walk the stress was less. Not gone, but not as bad.

By night, though, it had returned full force, and Tate was once again pacing like a caged animal in the confines of the cabin. I studied him and asked, "Can we light the woodburning stove?"

"Why?" He barked the question, then, realizing how he sounded, he repeated it in a softer voice. "Why now?"

"Because fire is relaxing, which is something you need badly."

The stove was an advanced model that burned its own smoke and the night was pitch black. "I guess we can chance it." He lit a fire that was soon burning brightly, with dancing shadows on the walls and heat radiating. More than those things, though, it did what I hoped it would do. It calmed him down. Somewhat.

We sat on the floor in front of the stove leaning against the couch with our legs draped over Noble who sprawled close to the fire. "He's going to burn up."

"He'll be okay. He likes heat."

We talked sporadically. For a while. Until silence was better than words and Tate's tension lessened. I watched it happen and rejoiced. And still we sat. Eventually the tension disappeared entirely. At last. I turned towards him, not to say anything, just to see how he was doing.

He was looking at me, head tilted a bit, eyes slitted in thought and something else, something I couldn't read. We said nothing, just examined each other minutely for a long time. Then he moved. Came close. He kissed me, slow and gentle, but I felt it in every fiber of my being.

As we parted, I said, "I thought we weren't going to let this happen because we don't know how we'll feel when it's over. When the telepathy thing goes away. If it does."

"You are right. We did come to an agreement. I believe I'm the one who suggested it and you said it was a good idea. Looking back, I'm sure we were both right because it was a wise move. It was the smart thing to do."

"So what changed?"

"Nothing. Everything. Doesn't matter what we said or what we agreed to, I'm only human and I'm hoping you are, too."

He came closer and we kissed again. Any onlooker would have said it was a chaste kiss, but it felt like a joining in which two separate beings became one. It was that deep. That consequential. And neither of us said anything about it, either out loud or telepathically. I didn't know what to make of this new thing that was happening because it was wonderful and scary and was both at the same time.

Was it telepathy? Or was it a natural extension of the unspoken connection between us? I didn't know. Was it love? Maybe, but maybe not. I'd never been in love so didn't know what it was like, and I suspected the same was true of Tate.

At that moment, Noble decided he was warm

enough and moved farther away from the heat. His move shoved our legs everywhere and we had to scramble to keep upright, and the effort ended the moment.

We put the fire out and went to bed.

As I pulled the covers up tight, I wondered what would have happened had Noble not acted like his usual self and done exactly the most inappropriate thing at the most inopportune moment. I decided I'd probably never know. I also decided that I had no idea whether the decision we'd made earlier about not allowing ourselves to get emotionally all tangled up was still valid, or whether time and circumstances had made it moot.

CHAPTER 18

Billy returned late the next morning with so much information that I guessed we'd spend the rest of the day listening. I made lemonade and we all grabbed huge frosted glasses of the delicious drink and adjourned to the porch because it was a lovely place to talk, but it turned out he had so many papers with him that needed to be spread over a table in order to see them correctly that we went inside and forgot lemonade and the lovely day and the porch and absolutely everything except the information he'd gleaned by talking with just about everyone connected with the weather forecasting business. Like Tate had said, he knew everyone.

"Weather For America is legit." No news there, we'd learned that online. "They are also rolling in money." That was news. "At first it looked like they'd filled a need that made the company very rich. And they did. Pin-point accurate weather forecasting is a sweet deal moneywise. But not enough to make them as rich as they are."

"Where does the extra money come from?"

"I was surprised, and so will you be. Or maybe you won't be surprised at all because the source of their recent infusion of capital comes from exactly where you'd expect it to come from. The same place most projects get tons of money that allow them to do all kinds of weird things."

Tate and I exchanged puzzled looks as Billy waited for us to figure it out for ourselves. It didn't take long. "The government?"

"Bingo."

"The government is funding research into telepathy?"

"Not telepathy. That must have been a side effect, and even now they might not know it happened to you guys. They were researching something else. Something that governments have wanted for generations but never succeeded at."

"What?" We were clueless.

"Weather warfare."

Tate struck his forehead. "And who better to figure out how to do that than a company that deals with weather in its daily business."

I continued with that train of thought. "A company that deals with pin-point accurate weather because a small storm would be preferred to a big one that could devastate an entire country, including places you'd not want destroyed."

"Small as in the kind that did a number on us."

"Yep, and the wind you experienced could have been their first attempt. An experimental gust that got out of control."

"And did so much damage they decided to discontinue the project."

"Or move the experimental stage to a place where weird, rogue storms won't be noticed."

I looked through the window at the miles of

wilderness. "Where?"

"Right where they are now without the overlook so no one can know what they are doing."

Billy hadn't spent much time at his cabin since buying it. As he said, it was more of a retirement place than a home for now. As he wrapped up his speech, we saw that he wanted to get reacquainted with his purchase. So, as he proceeded to examine it top to bottom and inch by inch, Tate and I took Noble and went outside to let him fall in love with his home all over again without interference.

Remembering how important invisibility was, we dressed in camouflage that I hadn't known existed until Tate pulled a couple of green and brown splotchy ponchos from somewhere and threw one in my direction. His fit well. Mine, even though it was smaller than his, hung almost to the ground. Noble was just Noble.

As soon as we were far enough away that Billy couldn't see us, Tate stopped. Waited for me to notice and return to where he leaned against a fir tree. His eyes slitted and there was something about him that brought me to full alert. A lazy smile that wasn't lazy at all. A gleam in his eyes that took in me and everything around me. My body tingled and I didn't know why. Or maybe I did.

"What's going on?" Telepathy because the wind in the pines was the only proper sound.

"It's nice here."

It was nice everywhere in the green and brown forest. *"Is something wrong?"*

"I need to do something. It'll only take a moment."
"What's wrong?"

He moved. Took my hands and pulled me close and soon we were continuing what we'd started the night before and I made no attempt at all to stop it or even slow it down. Because it felt right. It was right. Absolutely, totally, completely, and finally right.

When we came back to earth, I pulled far enough away to examine him. *"What about our deal?"*

He sighed and backed a bit farther away. *"Now we know what's going on, I realize we're in the middle of something bigger than I thought. Bigger than I could possibly have guessed."*

He stared at the sky behind me, the forest, and nothing in particular. *"The thing is, I don't know everything, I don't know what's going to happen next, I don't know how this will end. None of us do. So I suddenly felt a need to be with you. Hold you. Know we are good. Just in case."*

For all the reasons we'd agreed to keep emotions out of our relationship, I should have pulled away. But he was right. Things were getting scary. So instead of pulling away, I leaned into him. He was warm and smelled like pine needles and his body against mine was hard as nails. *"Me too. You."* Because right then I needed him badly. In addition to being the one man I wanted in my life he was a bulwark against all the bad things in the world.

He looked into my eyes. Stroked my face. *"I can't ask anything of you, not now, not with the future in doubt. And I can't say anything because the future could turn it into a lie. But that'll change. Some day we'll have options."*

"We'll have a life."

"A good life. I promise." Then he spoke out loud

for emphasis and because his next words were important. "And I keep my promises."

He kissed me then. Rather, we kissed each other for a long, long time. Then we moved apart and continued our walk with Noble. We climbed a hill from which we surveyed miles of unbroken forest in much the same way we'd looked over the valley before the rogue wind came. We stepped across a tiny stream that murmured its way towards somewhere unknown. Finally, we returned to Billy's cabin because we had to face reality, and not because we wanted to go back to what was tearing a hole in the fabric of our lives.

As we approached the cabin, Tate turned to me. "One thing." Said out loud because we were back in the real world. "If WFA hadn't played around with weather, I'd never have met you and I'm glad for that if not for anything else."

When we entered, we found Billy on a couch with his feet on a battered chest that served as a coffee table. He was waiting for us. The morning briefing hadn't been complete. "There's more, guys. You looked like you needed a break, and I hope you enjoyed your walk because I'm now going to tell you the rest of the story."

We dropped onto the second couch in the cabin, Tate sat first. He pulled me beside him and wrapped an arm around me. Billy's eyebrows rose, but he didn't comment though he did roll his eyes as we settled in and Tate asked, "What more can there be?"

"The second reason Weather For America is interested in controlling the weather instead of just predicting it."

"Are they working for someone else? Selling info to another country?"

"As far as I could discover, they are patriotic enough. But their business philosophy is to make as much money as possible no matter how they do it. In short, they are greedy, so they are working the project from all angles. Weather war for the government and weather manipulation for their own bottom line."

What Billy had found out was obvious. "They plan to create ideal weather for their clients, not just predict it. They plan to do so for a hefty price. Think of the implications for people who don't choose to sign with them or can't afford their services."

"There's only so much rain to command. So much sunshine."

"Which they will steal from others to give to their clients, and everyone else will get what's left over and end up going out of business."

"That's wrong."

"According to them it's just business, and because creating weather is new there aren't any laws to prevent them from doing whatever they choose."

"We must stop them. It's beyond just us now. We need to tell the government."

"That's not a good idea." Billy and Tate agreed. "They're smart enough to have a contact in the government that knows exactly what's going on and is helping them accomplish their goals. For a hefty price, of course." Tate pulled me closer. Held me tighter. "Someone with few morals who would be more than happy to see a couple of interlopers disappear forever."

"So what's next?" I asked the question but neither man answered.

CHAPTER 19

When I went to bed, the two men stayed up. I couldn't sleep so heard their voices late into the night though they spoke so low I couldn't understand the words, and Tate didn't use telepathy to let me know what they were talking about. The only thing I knew was that they didn't sound like a couple of guys talking over old times. No laughs. Whatever they discussed was dead serious.

The next morning, I learned what all the talk had been about. They had devised a plan. Billy explained. "I find out who the WFA contact is in the government and what their plans are now that their recent experiment went haywire."

I hoped he was right. "After we get to the bottom of things and alert someone with ethics as to what's going on, that person can find another company – a decent company – to replace WFA."

"Is that possible? WFA has a contract."

"Breaking the law, destroying property, and trying to kidnap private citizens should invalidate any contract."

"Good luck, but I won't hold my breath."

Billy sighed. "It'll take a while. I'm on an indefinite leave of absence. I said it was an emergency, which it is." He examined Tate and me. "It's dangerous for you two to do anything, so I'm the one who'll get stuff done right now. You two do your best to coexist peacefully in one small cabin in the middle of nowhere, and don't call attention to yourselves should you break out in an argument."

He left later that day after dropping more burner phones on the table so we could communicate. One call per phone, then destroy it, a precaution so extreme my stomach churned at the thought of the danger that meant. The fact that WFA was so well connected multiplied the danger a thousand times. I put the phones in a drawer where I wouldn't see them, leaving one out that Billy had said he'd use to contact us if such was necessary.

The only good thing was that we were in the middle of nowhere, like Billy had said. We were safe. We went for walks with Noble. I cooked the fish Tate caught in the nearby stream. We spent long hours on the porch before closing up the cabin. Each night I regretted having chosen the bed farthest from Tate because now I wanted to be near him. But I stayed where I was.

Every morning before doing anything else, Tate checked the backpacks he'd filled soon after arriving at the cabin. As soon as we were up and ready for the day, he'd check the contents that he'd checked the day before and then he stuffed them back into two backpacks. The next day he did the same. And the next. And so on. It was money and clothes mostly, though after Billy brought the burner phones, he added them.

Every morning I watched and finally asked, "Why?"

"It's best to be prepared."

"Aren't you over reacting? This place is safe."

"So far."

A full two weeks after Billy left the second time, one of the burner phones rang, the one still on the table because it was the one Billy would call from. We froze when the sound went through the cabin. It was the first time any phone had rung since we'd arrived. I stared at it as if it was poison.

Tate answered and nodded as he listened to someone I couldn't hear. His face grew taut, his body tense. When he put the phone down he said, "Time to go."

"Huh?"

"That was Billy. Someone didn't like the questions he was asking. They checked him out and are on their way here, so we've got to leave. Now." He moved as he spoke. "I'll get the backpacks. You find Noble and grab some food for him and for us because I don't know when we'll be able to stop. Then we're out of here."

I stood in confusion as what he'd said sank in. Then I moved. I ran to the kitchen and filled a couple bags with hands that shook, ran to the door and called Noble who, thankfully, was sleeping on the porch. By then Tate had gone to the loft, grabbed the backpacks, and returned. We both ran outside.

"We take one truck. The brown one because it's the most likely to be overlooked. We hope whoever is on their way doesn't know what we're driving or that we have two trucks. When they see one in the shed, they'll think we went for a walk and will wait for our return."

"That'll give us more time to get far from here."

"That's the idea." We threw everything into the back seat, and Noble climbed on top of it all. Then we left. "Hang on. This could be a rough ride."

I hoped Tate was a good driver. I figured he must be since he excelled at other macho type guy things and driving trucks qualified. But I prayed as we careened along the dirt road that was barely wide enough for the truck, scraping branches and bumping over rocks as we went.

We turned onto a county road and he speeded up even more until a vehicle appeared in the distance coming our way. Then he slowed to a sedate speed. "Get down. Whoever is after us is looking for a man and a woman. If this is our guy, I just want him to see another farmer in an errand truck."

It was a shiny black car with tinted windows. My heart pounded and I went as low as I could, dropping to my knees on the floor and scrunching into a ball. When the black car was in the rear view mirror, Tate said, "He's not slowing. Not turning around. So our little ruse worked or he's a local out for a morning drive."

I peered in the rear view window. "It's black and has tinted windows. It had to have been WFA."

"No logo, but I'd guess it was them because they turned onto the road to Billy's place, and only someone who knew about the cabin would even know it's a road. We got out just in time."

As soon as we were around next curve and could no longer be seen by the driver of the black car, Tate speeded up and we flew along the county road, raising dust and sending small animals scurrying for the safety of roadside bushes.

Then we reached the highway and merged with

traffic, and the tension in Tate's body eased. "So far, so good."

From the passenger seat I looked out the window and wondered if each vehicle we saw was looking for us. I wanted to duck each time. It got so bad that I had to tell myself not to be paranoid. The entire world wasn't after us. Just WFA.

Tate knew what I was thinking. "Being cautious isn't being paranoid. It's a survival skill."

When we reached a town large enough to have a decent shopping district, we had a topper installed over the bed of the pickup. Then we bought a mattress and bedding and put them there.

"We sleep in the truck from now on. No motels because we'd have to register, and no campgrounds for the same reason."

"If no campgrounds, where can we sleep?" The bed in the truck would be comfortable but it had to be parked somewhere.

"Truck stops, and we make sure there are as many large trucks between us and the highway as possible. In the middle of a bunch of over-the-road trucks is best. This truck is small enough to be hidden from view."

We bought a camp stove, and cooler, and everything else necessary to cook meals at wayside stops. I examined the stove and wondered how it worked. "I hope we find another place to stay soon."

Tate wasn't encouraging. "That could take a while." Tate, the most competent man I'd ever known, wasn't optimistic. That scared me more than I cared to admit. Billy's place seemed like a lovely dream.

Our first night involved getting used to sleeping in the back of the truck and next to each other with Noble sprawled across the front seat. I was closer to Tate than in the cabin where we were separated by the length of the loft, and closer even than in the honeymoon suite where we shared a bed that took up half the room. The only mattress that would fit the truck bed was a double bed size. Not even a queen. Just a double.

We had two sleeping bags. We started out with each of us having a bag, but it didn't work. The space was too cramped, the sleeping bags too thick. So we slept on top of one and under the second one. Tate slid into his side first and said ruefully, "Here's where we discover if we're compatible or not."

I laughed. The first laugh since so long ago that I couldn't remember when I'd last found something funny. It felt good. Later, after slowly and very carefully sliding in next to Tate, I was glad for the laughter because what I felt then was entirely different. New. And something I'd never admit to out loud. I was glad telepathy didn't include reading each other's feelings.

Or did it? There'd been times we might have mentally read each other's emotions, though each time could have been common sense instead of extrasensory perception. I slid far down into the sleeping bag and hoped no extrasensory ability had been involved those previous times because I didn't want Tate to be able to read my feelings at the moment. Or my thoughts, which were all about the man beside me.

He moved. His hand slid over my shoulder. I jumped a mile and hoped again that he hadn't read my emotions.

He hadn't. "Sorry." He pulled back and rolled away.

I felt awful. "Don't be sorry. I startle easily and was surprised. Not your fault." I wished he hadn't rolled away. I wanted his arm around me.

He rolled back towards me. Had he read my mind after all and knew what I wanted? I felt his smile in the darkness that had overtaken the world in the hours since finding a truck stop, picking a spot in the back row of trucks and cooking a meal on the grass that edged the concrete parking area. We'd eaten standing up. "Tomorrow we get a couple folding chairs."

"And a table."

"Guess we have a lot to learn about our new life."

He spoke quietly, inches away. "It's not a life I'd choose for any length of time." He sounded despondent. Not like the Tate I knew.

I wanted to be upbeat. I rolled towards him until we were face to face, though it was impossible to see each other in the dark. "We'll find another place." I touched his face. Traced the shape of it. "A wonderful place, and it'll be safe because no one will be able to connect it to either of us."

He sighed heavily and draped an arm across me, again, but this time it stayed. "Tomorrow we start looking for your fairytale place, but I'm not hopeful. We can't advertise our needs, and can't give our names to real estate agents, so it'll be a long search." He moved closer until we were as close together as it was possible to be. I wiggled until we fit perfectly.

We were possibly in the most precarious situation we'd known since the wind blew up the canyon and changed our lives forever. And yet that night I slept like a baby.

Sun slanting through the truck windows woke me

up the next morning early. For once Tate wasn't already up, but he was awake. He was staring at me. I blinked and met his look and we stayed that way for a long time, not speaking either out loud or telepathically. The sun moved enough that it no longer spotlighted us, instead waking Noble in the front seat. We heard the dog move until the sun no longer bothered him. Then he went back to sleep.

"When I got out of the Army, if anyone had told me that I'd be sleeping with a beautiful woman and her big, black dog before the summer was done, I'd have said they were insane."

"But here you are."

"Yes, here we both are, and can you guess what I want to do about it?"

"You want to not be chased?"

"That would be nice, I'll give you that. But it's not the most important thing at the moment."

"What is?"

"This."

If the sun had still been in my eyes, Tate would have blocked it when he rose and dropped enough to kiss me. Hard. Deep. Without warning. I had no time to raise a defense against my body's reaction to what I'd wanted so long that I almost didn't believe when it happened. It took seconds for me to come to my senses enough to pull my arms out from the sleeping bag and wrap them around him and return the kiss with everything I had.

CHAPTER 20

I don't know what would have happened next if Noble had stayed asleep. But he didn't, and he let us know in loud doggie fashion that he needed to go for a walk and he needed to go immediately.

Tate broke away and rolled onto his back and laughed. "A dog. My great love scene is stolen by a dog!"

I laughed too. "It happens."

He threw off the sleeping bag and shimmied into his jeans while lying flat. "I'll take him out and make breakfast. You can go back to sleep."

"I'm awake."

"You never wake early. Never."

I eyed him as he pulled a shirt over his head and couldn't figure how he managed in the tight quarters. "I'm not normally awakened by a knight in shining armor." Which, as I said the words, I realized was how I saw him. A knight. A savior. A very special man.

His eyes slitted. "Well, if you don't object, it's how you'll wake up every morning from now on."

Something in me moved. Warmed. "From now on is vague. How long, exactly?"

He stopped. Smoothed his shirt. Looked away and then back. "As long as you're okay with it." He took a deep breath. "I hope forever."

Silence came over us. Even Noble was quiet. "Forever and a day."

He came down again. Kissed me again. Gently. Then not gently at all. Then Noble barked and he moved away from me and opened the back of the truck and climbed out. "Later. We'll talk later." He and Noble went for a walk as I rolled over, grabbed my clothes, and tried my best to dress underneath a sleeping bag while wondering what had just happened. Had we agreed to what I thought we'd agreed to?

He returned in a half hour. By then the truck stop was filled with the sound of diesel trucks roaring to life and leaving one by one. The truck was soon exposed so we got on the road as soon as possible and didn't stop until we found a tiny dirt road that turned off the highway and headed for what must be no place at all. We cooked and ate sitting on a log until we couldn't stand it any longer. Until the not talking got to us both. Tate put his plate on the ground. I did the same.

"So how about it? Marry me?" I didn't have time to say anything before he added, "Provided we get out of this alive."

"Of course I'll marry you."

He pulled me close, and I knew that, yes, we did experience each other's emotions, though I didn't know if it was a special sense that came with telepathy or was what every couple feels when together, but I knew as surely as I knew my name that what we were feeling was love and not the effects of mind-to-mind communication.

"Marriage requires a license."

"Which can be traced."

"And a waiting period."

"During which someone could find us."

He nodded. "Another reason to take WFA down. So we can get started with the life I didn't know I wanted until I met you."

He ruffled my hair. I wanted to do the same with his dark, thick hair but didn't because he might be embarrassed. Or maybe he'd like it. I didn't know. How much I had to learn! Would our lives last long enough to learn that and a million other things? I'd settle for just a reasonable amount of time and a dozen things to do during that time. A handful of things, and a small amount of time.

We packed our cooking things and prepared to return to our life on the run. I looked around. No one had come along the dirt road. "It's probably not used much if at all."

Tate agreed. "We should look for a place like this. Isolated. Not worth a second glance." We drove to the end of the road, hoping we'd find such a place. No such luck. All we found was a cabin in ruins already returning to the forest.

Then the burner phone rang again. I answered. It was Billy. "What say we meet somewhere so I can get you guys caught up on what's going on?"

We agreed, and two days later we met Billy in a local park on the edge of another of the hundreds of small towns we'd been through. A group of school kids were there planting trees, and Noble wanted to join them. I knew few trees would get planted with him around so we stayed on the other side of the park.

Billy admired our living arrangements. I told him he was insane if he thought it was a decent way to live.

He laughed and said he'd made some small progress in Washington so our vagabond days wouldn't be forever.

"Not everyone in government is corrupt, and I found a couple who aren't, but it'll take a while for them to figure out how to shut down WFA without ending the research they are doing into weather warfare. The Pentagon is very interested in it."

"Why don't they just transfer the project to some other company?"

"WFA has the data, and they are keeping it to themselves. They say they don't yet have anything to report. Not true, but no one can prove it."

"They've made progress. Look what happened to us."

"I couldn't tell them you two became telepathic. All I could say was that two people were endangered by WFA's illegal methods, so WFA is trying to silence you. That's enough to get WFA defunded. They're looking into it, but they don't believe WFA is trying to take you out just because you were in a bad storm. So it's a low priority."

Tate raked his hair. "So we wait."

"We won't tell anyone about the telepathy."

Just then Noble slipped out of his collar and went as fast as he could run to the school kids that he knew would give him hugs and part of their lunches. I ran after him, and Billy followed. "Kids and a dog. I want to watch."

The school kids loved Noble even more than they loved planting trees. Their teacher loved him too, thankfully. Billy winked at me, and I was enjoying this unexpected normal moment in life when suddenly, Noble left the kids. Came to me. Looked past me. And started to growl.

Before I could stop him, he was gone, running back to Tate as fast as he could go.

A feeling so powerful it almost dropped me to my knees hit me in the solar plexus. I doubled over and held my middle with both hands.

"Run!" It was Tate. *"They found us! They are here!"*

Noble reached Tate as two huge men dragged him into a car with its engine running. The large Lab flew at them. Grabbed one and held on tight, but a third man drew a gun and shot. Noble cried, twisted in the air, and fell. By the time he could get back up, the car door had slammed and the car had peeled out of the park on two wheels.

"Don't come after me! Stay safe! I love you! Then, like a light blinking out, he went silent. I called to him, screaming telepathically, but there was no response. Nothing. No sense of him at all.

The kids and their teacher were in a state of shock. Noble was limping. Billy and I ran to him and checked him over. "Just a graze. He'll need some care, but he'll live." He stared towards where the car had disappeared, swearing silently, and lifted Noble into the car. "Can you talk to Tate?"

"Nothing." I told him about Tate's last words.

His eyes narrowed and for a moment he resembled Tate. Same focus. Same determination. "Think he's alive?"

I folded over and forgot how to breathe. "I don't know. I just know that one second we were talking, and the next he was gone. Totally. It's never happened before. We've always been aware of each other even when we aren't talking telepathically." Something I now realized I'd taken for granted. I'd not known it was happening. It just *was*. Now I knew the sensing Tate and I had always wondered about really existed. We truly did have some kind of connection. And that connection had just been broken.

"We'll assume he's alive and unconscious because he's of no use to them dead."

Or they were eliminating a potential problem and Tate was half the problem. The most dangerous half. "We have to do something."

Billy reached out. Touched me. "We'll get him back. Don't think otherwise. But first we have to find out where they're taking him."

Billy climbed into his car, and I followed in the truck with Noble in the passenger seat. He was in pain but was still the dog that had recognized Mike Dickens for what he was. Evil incarnate. Instead of his usual feed-me, love-me, pet-me demeanor, he was now the dog that had just seen an enemy and tried to take him out.

Billy wasn't into camping. We chose a motel and registered under assumed names. Two rooms because, as he explained, we were business partners, not lovers. "It wasn't a lie. We are partners," he said later over dinner in the attached café. "Just not the kind of business most people work at."

We adjourned to my room afterwards where we cleaned Noble's wound and applied antibiotic and a bandage that covered half his body so he'd not tear it off. So Billy was present when it happened.

"Hi, Zoe. I love you and I'm awake."

CHAPTER 21

I swooned in relief. I shouted to Billy. "He's alive! Tate is alive." Then to Tate, telepathically, *"What happened? Are you hurt?"*

"Can he think clearly?" I nodded. Billy slumped in relief. "Thank God." I told him what Tate had said. "Does he know where he is?"

He didn't. He was blindfolded. They thought he was still unconscious. *"I'll try to figure out where I'm being taken."* They didn't know we were telepathic. They didn't know we could communicate. It was our one advantage.

Billy said, "Now we can make plans."

Tate kept us informed but didn't recognize from sounds what road he was on. Until much later, still pretending to be unconscious, he was carried into a building and dumped onto a bed. When whoever carried him there left, he got up, pulled off the sack covering his head and looked around. Walked the room. *"I'm in the WFA facility. I can see the ridge where we stood when the wind came up the canyon. There's a cot and not much else. It has a window, but it has bars."*

"Are you okay?"

"I feel okay."

"Ask if he knows who took him or what they

want."

I asked and then relayed Tate's response. "He doesn't know. He hasn't seen anyone yet." I was still giddy with the knowledge that he was alive.

"Someone is coming. If there's a way for this telepathy thing to let you hear what they are saying, I'll do it."

Soon I heard the sound of a door opening. I heard it because Tate heard it and somehow sent the sound to me. Then I heard someone's voice. I closed my eyes to hear better and relay the conversation to Billy, who was listening closely, brows knit, features tight, ready to do battle with the devil in order to free his friend.

It was Mike Dickens. He spoke, and I heard his words through Tate. *"That first visit all I wanted was a little information. If you two had been open about what had happened to you none of this would be necessary. So it's your fault that you're here."*

Tate replied. *"We told you what happened. Now if you'll let me go, we'll forget this whole unfortunate incident happened. I won't press charges."*

Mike spoke again. *"Sorry, but that's not possible. There are people here who don't believe nothing happened, and they want to find out precisely what that wind – that little laboratory accident -- did to you two."*

"So it wasn't intentional?"

A sigh. *"No, and if you'll just be honest about what happened, this unfortunate incident will end quickly."*

"We were almost blown to smithereens, that's what happened. But we survived. Like we told you before, only you refused to believe us."

"There were things – chemicals – in that wind, one

of which has the ability to change any person it touches. Any human. So you see, you two accidentally became our test subjects, and we can't let you just walk away without learning what happened." He laughed. *"Nice of you to volunteer. Now we don't have to worry about the legal aspects of experimenting on humans. In fact, no one needs to know about you two. Just me and a couple others."*

"WFA owns this place. They'll know."

There was a laugh. *"No they won't. This is a little side project of mine that WFA knows nothing about that will make me exceedingly rich if the tests show what I'm hoping. That the chemical changed you two. I believe you both are now enhanced. Different. Special."*

"What kind of tests? How are we supposed to be enhanced?"

"We think you already know and just aren't telling. But the tests will tell us everything, whether you want us to know or not."

"When will you do the tests?"

"As soon as it can be arranged." There was a pause. *"We weren't prepared, so it might take a few days. Then you can go home."* Another pause. *"If you survive, that is. You might not."*

I almost puked. *"He's going to kill you."*

There was the sound of a door slamming and a lock being turned as Mike Dickens left.

Tate spoke. *"Tell Billy everything Mike said."*

"Will do, and I love you."

"Me too, you. I love you, and when I get out of this place I plan on doing something about it. And I will get out. Ignore what Mike said. He's an idiot."

Then he added, *"In the meantime, I'm exhausted.*

Whatever they gave me has after-effects. I'm barely staying awake, and I suspect that whatever Billy has in mind will need me to be fully functional, and I'm sure he has something planned."

"Go to sleep."

I told Billy what had transpired. His response was to nod slightly and pull out still another burner phone and place a call. When he flipped it shut, he said, "They'll be on their way first thing in the morning. They'll meet us at the café in Montclair, so we get going early tomorrow."

"Who's 'they?'"

"Friends. Former military, but they have skills that will be useful when the time comes." He looked at me thoughtfully. "When we take care of things. While you are staying far away where it's safe."

"I'm coming."

"Tate would kill me if anything happened to you."

"You need me. I can talk with Tate. Tell you what he knows. What he sees. What's going on inside WFA."

Billy gave a big sigh. "Okay. You're right. You're part of the group."

We set off for Montclair the next morning and reached the café around lunchtime. Once inside, Billy commandeered a table large enough for a family. He told the waitress, "There will be five in all." Three more military types.

Would four soldiers plus non-military me be sufficient? I slid into a chair and told the waitress I'd order later. I didn't say I needed time to decompress from what had happened and mentally prepare for what was to come, but I think Billy knew. We drank coffee while we waited.

When the other three arrived, they came straight to the table and dropped into chairs without speaking, nodding to Billy and me. Billy introduced them. "Ron, Benjamin, and Carlos." They nodded again, but still said nothing.

I discretely looked them over. Not quite clones of Tate or Billy, but there was a similarity. Muscular, erect posture, relaxed on the outside but not on the inside. Ron was blonde and the shortest of the group, Benjamin was wiry with an intellectual look about him, and Carlos was Mexican-American with olive skin and liquid eyes women everywhere would swoon over.

"Is it okay to talk here?" Ron looked around the crowded café.

"Probably not, but Zoe's house is most likely being watched."

Ron shrugged. "Let's eat here, and then go to her place. We can check it out. Make sure it's safe. We know how to look it over and take care of anyone who shouldn't be there."

We had hamburgers and fries, three each for the guys, one for me, and one to give Noble who waited in the truck. We asked for pop in cans that we drank on the way. Noble ate his hamburger in one swallow and wagged his tail in thanks as I led the small convoy to the house I thought I'd never see again.

Tate was in on the planning, with me relaying what was said so everyone knew what was going to happen. The newcomers said nothing when we explained how I could communicate with Tate. Benjamin raked his fingers through his hair, but the others didn't show their thoughts. I wondered how hard it was for them to keep their faces straight.

Noble didn't like being ignored. He tugged his bed to the middle of the action, begged scraps of food from everyone, and went to sleep. He thought he was the center of attention.

The guys spent the next day unloading supplies they'd brought. Explosives. Rifles. Handguns. Knives. Watches. Night vision goggles. And more. The sight of all those things set my body thrumming. This was real. Dangerous. Deadly. We sat in the living room, and wordlessly waited for night.

When it was dark enough, we left. I told Noble to guard the house. He wagged his tail and tugged his bed to his favorite spot between the living room and the kitchen, and then promptly fell sleep.

We headed for the WFA building in the canyon in three vehicles, and we kept the headlights on when we started, then doused them as we neared WFA. It was a new moon, really dark, and we were dressed all in black, with an extra black outfit for Tate. If anyone had seen us, they'd have called 911 and reported us as terrorists.

The building appeared empty. Two guards patrolled the perimeter, with a third in the hall outside Tate's room. We knew this because Tate had seen him as Mike Dickens came and went.

Tate had ascertained that the few scientists in the building occasionally worked late, and that seemed to be the case that night because there were several cars still in the parking lot when we arrived. We debated whether to wait until they left. Tate thought some people were about ready to leave. *"I hear people moving and footsteps. Sounds like they are going towards the main door."*

As we watched, three men left the building and crossed the parking lot, so the decision was made to proceed as soon as they were gone. Then a black car came down the road and passed us, going towards WFA. We were parked off the road behind bushes, so should be well hidden in the darkness. We held our collective breath, but the car continued on and turned into WFA, pulling to a stop near the men who were leaving.

They spoke with whomever was in the car. Then they all headed back towards the building instead of leaving as we'd expected.

"Too many people?" Billy asked me to relay the information to Tate, while the others digested this unexpected turn of events. "Should we cancel?"

Tate was confident we could handle things. I relayed his message. "That's four civilians who are inside, plus three guards, two of whom are outside. Tate doesn't hear enough sounds to indicate more people. He thinks it's very doable."

The group agreed. Piece of cake. So we scattered according to our prearranged plan. My job was to stay back and keep in contact with Tate. I wasn't to take any chances because without me, there'd be no communication with Tate. I thought there might be a touch of macho protection of the fragile female in that decision, but their reasoning was sound. I was telepathic. They weren't.

I'd relay Tate's messages via cell phone much the same way a family might gossip in a group chat. The whole operation was planned in minute detail.

I put on my night vision goggles, found a spot with

a clear line of sight to the WFA building, patted the Glock in my pocket, and settled in to do my part.

CHAPTER 22

I contacted Tate. *"We're here. Be ready."*

"Got an extra weapon? In case I decide to use it on a certain someone who thinks he's going to get rich off us." I giggled, and Tate laughed. Then we waited.

He spoke soon. *"The guys are outside the window. They are working on the bars. I'm getting out of here!"* Less than a minute later he was exultant. *"I'm out!"* Then he spoke in a different voice. His I'm-going-to-take-care-of-you voice. *"We can take it from here. Thanks for telling me what was going on. You can go back to the SUV. Wait for me there. Stay safe."*

I wasn't brave. I was the opposite of brave. But I wasn't about to become an onlooker. It was my fight too, and the need for justice was a hot poker through my inner self. So I stayed where I was, looking down on the WFA research building. If things went wrong, I'd do something. I wouldn't make things worse by doing something stupid, getting caught, and having to be rescued. But the Glock in my pocket was loaded, and I knew how to use it.

The team went about their assigned tasks. They were dark figures on one side of the building, barely seen in the moonless night, but I knew the plan so I knew where to look.

There was movement. A brief scuffle. They'd taken out the first of the outside guards. The poor guy was out for the count and was soon dragged away from the building.

Then the team moved to the other side of the building for the second guard. I couldn't see what happened but when they reappeared and headed for the front entrance, I figured the second guard was also out of business. They were ready for the main event.

"We're in the lab." Tate kept me informed. *"We're laying explosives."* Moments later he said, *"There won't be enough left of this building to fill a garbage can."*

They were setting small explosives timed to go off in sequence as they moved through the building, starting with the laboratory. The explosives would start fires that would engulf the entire building.

Soon after, the first explosion appeared at the far end of the building. Then another. And another. Soon the entire building was on fire. It was exactly as planned, and in no time the entire building was a pillar of fire.

Five figures ran out of the main door. Not Tate's team, the running men were the one's we'd first seen in the parking lot, plus the one guarding Tate's room. But they didn't leave. Instead, they took rifles from the trunk of one of the cars, plus pistols that they stuffed into their pockets. Then they stationed themselves on either side of the main door. Waiting. Watching. Because they knew someone was inside and had set the building on fire and would be coming out soon.

I grabbed my cell phone. "Don't use the main entrance. There are men with guns!" I used the cell phone so the whole team could hear. But my call was for nothing. The phone was dead. Interference from the explosions? I didn't know why, but all that mattered was that I had to get a message to the team.

I mentally screamed at Tate. *"There are men with rifles at the main entrance."*

"Got it. Thanks. I'll tell the others." Which meant he'd not leave until everyone else was safely out. Typical Tate.

A dark figure climbed through a side window and ran towards the surrounding forest. One team member and he was safely out. Then another headed towards the trees from a different exit. And another and another. Until Tate was the only one still inside.

I mentally screamed at Tate. *"Don't go out the front door. They're waiting for you."*

"Doesn't matter. I have to get out, and that's the only way. This place is about to blow sky high."

He'd be walking into an ambush. I had to do something. I had to help.

Pulling the Glock from my pocket, I sprinted down the hill towards the building, screaming as I ran. "I'm here, you cowards! Come get me!" The only thing I could think to say because words weren't important. Getting their attention was all that mattered, so they'd redirect their firepower towards me instead of Tate.

It was dark, I was a moving target and pretty far away. I told myself they'd miss, and hoped I was right.

They stopped. Turned. And came at me at a dead run, rifles lifted and ready to fire as soon as they got a good target. I fired my Glock blindly, hoping the realization that I had a gun would slow them down, so I could turn back and run for the protection of the trees. It wasn't much of a plan, but it was all I had.

They kept coming but didn't fire because I wasn't a decent target. Yet.

But Billy and the rest of the team had heard my shots, too, and my yelling, and knew what I was doing. I saw movement from the corner of my eye. Dark figures returning from the woods where they'd run. Then I heard shots.

One of the men coming at me fell, screaming. The others scattered, but by then the team was closing in and had them boxed in. The thugs slowed, turning one way and then another, unsure which was the more dangerous, the person on the hill with a gun, or the ones coming after them who also had guns.

One made a break for it and was shot. He, too, screamed and threw down his weapon as the remaining thugs debated which way to run.

"Drop your weapons." Billy's voice echoed in the night. He wasn't the Billy I'd come to know. He was authority in a black hoodie. The men obeyed.

"They have pistols," I called from the hill.

The team closed in. "Keep your hands up, and don't move an inch or you'll regret it."

Two of the team checked the men who were down while those still standing were patted for weapons as Billy held a rifle on them. "No life-threatening injuries."

"We'll call 911 on our way out and tell them there's a fire and that they'll find the arsonists tied up neatly nearby," Billy said.

Zip ties came out, and soon the WFA men were trussed 'like pigs at a market,' as Benjamin eloquently put it.

I wanted to run to Tate and never let him go. I wanted to do a thousand things. Instead I stuck the Glock back in my pocket, walked over to where he stood, and simply leaned into him.

"I was so afraid for you."

"Me?! You were worried about me? You're the one who made herself a target. I thought I'd lose you. I've never been so scared in my life."

"It's over."

Tate put me fractionally away from his warm, solid body. "I'm afraid it's not quite over."

"What do you mean?"

"Mike Dickens isn't one of the men nicely tied up for the authorities."

Billy came to where we stood. "We'll get him. Someday, somewhere, we'll get him."

The team called 911 as we reached the highway on our way back to the Cape Cod. Then Billy threw away the last burner phone after wiping off any fingerprints and smashing it to bits. "Too much hassle if they trace the call. Too much paperwork."

I was totally drained as I sat in the back seat with Tate's arm around me. I couldn't stop shivering and didn't think I'd be able to walk the short distance from the SUV to the Cape Cod. "Don't worry," he said with a smile that I could feel more than see. "I'll carry you."

When we reached the Cape Cod, though, someone was already there, on the porch with Noble, except Noble's ears were flat against his head, the hair on his back was up, and a low growl came from his throat. "Noble! What are you doing?!"

I was about to tell Noble he was a bad dog when Tate went close enough to identify the man. He began to laugh. He bent over and slapped his knees and called the rest of the team over. "Guys, meet Mike Dickens."

Noble never had liked Mike and the man now cowered against the wall, afraid to take a step in any direction lest my vicious dog take a bite out of him.

Tate went up to Mike. "Nice to see you, Mike."

"Get that dog away from me."

"Who? Noble? Why? He's a good doggie, though he does get protective when people try to break into his home." Tate patted Noble before turning back to Mike. "Is that what you were doing, Mike? Breaking in?"

Mike blustered. "Of course not. I came to see Zoe, and this monster attacked me." He continued with more bluster. "I'm going to report this to the authorities. When I get back to WFA, I'll call the law, and you'll wish you'd never been born."

Tate laughed more. "Sorry, Mike, but the WFA research facility burned to the ground less than an hour ago."

"That can't be true." Mike sagged.

"The entire building is gone, including the laboratory, all the paperwork, and all the computers. Everything."

Mike's eyes narrowed. "You destroyed private property. You'll spend the rest of your life in jail."

"I doubt that," Tate said easily, pulling something from his pocket. The cell phone he'd been given by the team when they broke him free of the building. The one that hadn't worked when I called. I wondered if it worked now. "Not when I play the recordings I made when you threatened me." He waved it in the air. "Want me to play it now so you'll know exactly what charges you'll soon face?"

Mike caved. "You're insane." He knew he was beaten, but bluster was in his personality. "I'm leaving this place." He took a step, looking towards Noble to see if the dog would let him go. Tate patted Noble so he'd know it was okay to let Mike pass.

As Mike reached his car he called back. "Charging me won't work. I have friends."

"Some of whom are now in custody and will rat you out in exchange for reduced sentences."

Mike climbed in his car and peeled out of the driveway.

"Did you really have a cell phone, and did you really record the conversations?"

"No but Mike Dickens doesn't know that."

"Do you think he'll come after us?"

Tate shrugged. "He knows he's done, and so is his project."

"I don't want to live in fear."

Tate inspected Noble. "No need to worry. You've got Noble."

I smiled and couldn't stop smiling. "And you. I've got you."

His reply was immediate and emphatic. "Yes, you do have me, and I've got you. Now and forever

EPILOGUE

Having a policeman for a father turned out to be a plus when Tate and I explained the whole thing to my parents. We told them everything, from the telepathy, to the end of the WFA research facility, and our part in it. My mother's eyes went wide. My father's narrowed for a while, but all he did was nod and welcome Tate to the family.

Tate's family consisted of Billy, Benjamin, Ron, and Carlos and they were there when we got married in a simple ceremony in my parents' back yard. I appreciated that they restrained themselves afterward and didn't relate a single gory story about their lives in and after being in the military. They were perfect gentlemen.

Noble was there, of course, begging treats from everyone. He spent the next day throwing up, and my parents had to deal with him while Tate and I took a brief honeymoon.

We simply got in a car and set out with no particular destination in mind. But one thing we agreed on. "No honeymoon suites." Because we remembered the first night in the honeymoon suite in the motel when we were on the run.

"It was awful."

"Worse than awful. But the worst part was being next to you and not doing anything about it. I guarantee that won't happen ever again."

"I didn't know."

Tate sighed. "You have no idea how hard it was."

"Yes I do." Because I knew how hard it had been for me. "We're married now."

After a week of meandering through the countryside, staying at quaint motels and eating at whatever café we happened upon, we picked up a recovered Noble and went home to the Cape Cod.

The first morning back, Tate checked it over to see what more was needed in the way of fixer-upper repairs. When he was finished with the inspection, he sighed. "I have about ten years' worth of work ahead of me."

"If I'd known you'd be part of my life, I might have bought a different house."

"I'd go crazy without something to do. I like work."

And I enjoyed watching him work. Actually, I enjoyed watching him do anything, which was good because I planned to spend the rest of my life watching him, being alive with him, loving him, and being loved back.

After making a list of supplies for the first batch of repair work, we headed for Montclair and then beyond, to the next town, because it had an actual lumberyard. We bought two-by-fours, and paneling, and paint, and the clerk couldn't understand why we didn't argue about what color to choose or even discuss options.

We didn't explain that we'd had a really spirited discussion about what color the front door should be.

He just couldn't hear us. I'll never get used to the fact that other people can't hear what Tate and I are saying.

We settled for a dull orange and both agreed it was perfect, but the poor clerk hesitated before mixing the color because he couldn't believe we knew what we wanted and feared we'd return it. We wouldn't.

We had lunch in a local café where the waitress' frown said we must be having a really bad day because we never said a word to each other during the entire meal. Not that she could hear.

She tried her best to engage us in conversation, beaming brightly to demonstrate how to be happy. We gave her a big tip because she was so concerned and caring and worked so hard to make us smile. She must have feared we'd had an argument and decided it was her mission in life to get us together again. When we left the café, arms around each other, she beamed with the pride of a job well done.

We stopped at the turn into the road Tate had discovered that in the future would suffice as an overlook since the one I'd grown to love no longer existed. We stayed for a long time, Tate's arms around me, with my back against his chest as we gazed over miles of forest spreading out below, but eventually we left because we couldn't stay forever.

When we got home, we stored the lumber in the garage where it would be easy to access. Then we went inside. I thought this would officially be the beginning of the rest of our lives. The day I'd remember forever for that reason. But before I could set my emotional clock for our future life, Tate spoke in a rather odd tone of voice. "There's something I want you to see."

"What?" I couldn't imagine what he was talking

about.

"I'll get it." He headed upstairs. When he returned, he held something small and black in his hand.

"That's what you want to show me? A stick drive? For a computer?'

"Yep."

"What's on it?"

"I don't know."

"How can you not know what's on it?"

"There wasn't time to do more than grab it and run."

The world stopped as I realized where this was headed. "Are you saying it's from the WFA research building? The one you blew up?"

"Yep. The one that burned to the ground."

"With everything in it. All its secrets."

"Except what's on this stick drive. If any secrets are on it. If they aren't gone forever."

He went to the desk in a corner and inserted the stick drive into my laptop. As he waited for the screen to light up, he explained. "As we were setting the explosives in the lab, I noticed a computer. It was in the middle of the lab and had this in it. Stick drives are small. It fit in my pocket. So I grabbed it. When we got back to the Cape Cod, I put it in the empty bedroom upstairs."

"And you don't know what's on it."

"I don't have a clue. But it just might be the formula for what happened to us."

"The formula Mike Dickens thinks is lost forever."

"Or it could be a totally trivial list of nothing important."

"But you don't think so."

"The computer was in the middle of the lab. It was on the only desk in there. Right where someone could use it when something important needed to be recorded."

The screen lit up. "Numbers. Symbols. They are incomprehensible. I don't have a clue what they mean."

"Neither do I, but they don't look trivial. They look beyond important."

"What should we do with it?"

We stared at one another until Tate spoke. "For now, I believe we should do nothing. But some day, after everything has settled down and we're positive no one is watching us or looking for us, maybe when that day comes, we should find someone who can explain all those numbers and symbols and find out if it's what we think it is."

"How will we find such a person?"

We both said his name at the same time. "Billy."

"He knows everyone. He'll find the right person and make sure that person can be trusted." He removed the stick drive and held it high. "In the meantime, it can go right back upstairs."

"When you work on the upstairs bedrooms, will you by any chance build a special place to hide it? A place where no one will find it until we want them to?"

He grinned. "Yep. Just like in the movies."

And that was the end of our conversation.

But some day it'll happen. Tate will contact Billy. Billy will find a scientist. And we'll find out what all those numbers and symbols mean.

It'll be interesting.

THE END

Hi,

I hope you enjoyed *Talk To Me*. If you want to see what else I've written, check out my website at http://www.FlorenceWitkop.com

My next book is *Guarding Brynn*. It's also a sweet, clean and wholesome, small town romance with a healthy dose of action and adventure, though there's nothing supernatural in it or anything even close. It's just a good page-turning, edge-of-your-seat adventure romance.

You can read the beginning of *Guarding Brynn* here. It'll be published by Winged Publications in the near future, will be available on Amazon, and will be free with Kindle Unlimited. Now, here's the beginning of *Guarding Brynn*.

GUARDING BRYNN

by

Florence Witkop

CHAPTER 1

Something had happened. Something bad. There was no other explanation for his lateness. My father was never late. Ever. You could set your clock by his comings and goings. He should be there already and there was no place to stop between where he'd called and the cabin.

It was a ten minute drive from the main road, and he'd called as he turned off of it onto our gravel road. He'd asked me to get steaks out of the refrigerator. "Cell service from here on is spotty so I called while I still could."

The family cabin was in an isolated area. Sometimes we had service, most of the time we didn't, and since my father loved steak he'd wanted to make sure they were done right, and since they were best if grilled at room temperature he'd wanted me to get them out before he arrived. He'd almost apologized for calling. But he was hungry.

I'd heard a car about ten minutes after that call so at first I'd thought it was my father, but it continued on past our cabin, so it wasn't him. I'd waited a few more minutes, expecting his car to turn into the driveway. When it didn't happen, I became a bit concerned. Another ten minutes and I was seriously concerned. Another ten and I got out the rain gear to go looking for him.

I'd need the gear. It was night and a storm outside was building to a crescendo. There was no moon, no stars. But the worst of the storm hadn't yet hit, so I could still walk along the road and look for him. But if I waited until the worst of the storm hit, the walk would be difficult and muddy, and it would have to be a walk because he had the only car. Mine was in the city.

I knew the road. I could walk the distance, even though it was night and the storm would make the darkness worse. Pretty much like in horror stories. But the distance itself wasn't great. So I grabbed boots, and a poncho, and a flashlight, and set off.

Surely I'd meet him on the road and get the car seat wet when he gave me a ride back, but he'd just roll his eyes and ask why I didn't wait a bit longer before getting all tied up in emotional knots and going out in a storm. Then he'd admit he was glad I did even though it wasn't necessary. He was that kind of father.

Never mind that he'd made a fortune and we were richer than my parents had dreamed possible when they were first married, and had got richer still as the years passed because he kept making money. Lots of money. But he was my dad, and that was all that mattered at the moment. I couldn't bear the thought of anything happening to him.

I pointed the flashlight ahead as I walked, watching for headlights. Didn't happen. It was just a black night that grew even blacker as the worst of the storm hit, with wind and rain that was a river of water falling from the sky.

When I reached an area where huge trees met overhead, the rain was less but the darkness was worse. It was so intense I could feel it. And still I saw no headlights and heard no car engine. Panic nibbled at the edges of my mind. I was almost at the highway.

Then I saw a dim glow ahead at the side of the road. I breathed a sigh of relief as I broke into a run because he'd clearly had engine trouble. We'd have to walk to the cabin and call for a tow truck, but we'd laugh about it afterwards.

Except when I reached the car, it wasn't my father's. It was an older SUV with no one inside. I opened the door hoping to find out why it was empty and where my father was. The dome light lit up the surrounding area somewhat.

"Hey!" A voice cut through the dark, and I backed out of the SUV and looked for the owner of the shout.

"You, there! On the road. In the car."

"What?" I saw nothing through the rain that fell faster and harder with each passing minute. "Who's calling? I can't see you."

"Down here. He's hurt. I need help."

"Who's hurt?" But, with a sinking heart, I knew who was hurt. My father. "Where are you?"

"At the bottom of the hill." I followed the voice and both clambered and slid down the embankment on the side of the road, and there, in the mud, was my father's car with someone pulling at the driver's side door trying to open it. It was crumpled and stuck. "Can you help? Maybe if we both pull it'll come open."

Together we pulled as hard as we could and slowly, with the metal protesting loudly, we got it open. "Dad!" I reached for him.

"Is he breathing?" The voice by my side was calm and collected.

I leaned as close as possible and put my ear to his chest. "Yes."

"Are you a nurse or a doctor?" I shook my head. "I'm not either, but I've had some experience with trauma. Want me to take a look?"

I backed away and let him take my place, wrapping my arms around my waist as I started to shake. My father was hurt and I couldn't see how bad, but he wasn't speaking. He wasn't conscious.

"His pulse is strong and his breathing is normal." The man who'd found my father turned to me. "Can I use your flashlight?"

In the light my father looked normal except for a streak of blood across his forehead. And the fact that he wasn't conscious. "A concussion?" He pointed the beam lower. One leg was at an odd angle. "It's broken. If that's the worst that happened, he'll be okay. I don't know about the gash on his forehead, though."

My father moved. Opened his eyes and blinked in the bright light. He moved again and groaned. The man who'd found him said, "Take it easy. Don't try to move. We'll get you to a hospital." He turned back to me. "Call 911 and ask for an ambulance."

I tried to call but shook my head. "No cell service." The worst time for no service.

He swore. "Then we'll have to take him ourselves. That's my SUV on the side of the road, but we have to get him up the hill and into it." He paused, finally seeing me now the first phase of the emergency was past and there was time to think past the immediate moment. "You're his daughter, aren't you? I heard you call him 'Dad.'" I said I was, and he asked, "Can you do this? Can you do what needs to be done even if he cries out? It can be hard for a family member to see someone they love in pain."

"I can do whatever is needed." If I'd come upon my dad alone, I'd be doing everything myself. "And thank you for stopping." Then I asked what I hadn't thought about until then. "Do you know what happened?"

"I do." The voice that had been concerned turned grim. "He was run off the road by a driver that didn't stop and didn't render aid. He didn't even slow down. Just kept going."

"I heard a car pass a while back. That must have been it."

"Did you see it? The color? Anything that will identify it when we go to the police?"

"Nothing. I only noticed because I was waiting for my dad and it came along at the right time."

My father groaned again and reached for me. "Brynn. Is that you?"

"It's me, Dad."

"I hurt. What happened?"

"You had an accident, but we'll get you to the hospital." How seriously was he hurt? How would we get him up the hill? I pushed a growing fear to the back of my mind and took his hand. "Don't worry, Dad. We'll take care of you."

He looked beyond me to the man who'd come along at the right time. "Who are you, and can you help us?"

"I'm Jace Browne and it'll be a piece of cake, but we need your cooperation. We need to get you up the hill and into my SUV. Then you can sleep all the way to town."

My father nodded. "Okay." He looked around, willing himself to full consciousness bit by bit as seconds ticked away. "Tell me what to do."

"Your leg is broken. Before we do anything else, I want to splint it."

"I'm cold." My father shivered.

Jace Browne spoke low. "He's going to go into shock pretty soon, so we have to do this as quickly as possible. I'm going to the other side of the car to tend to his leg. You stay here and hold the flashlight." He examined me. "Can you do that?"

"I can do whatever I have to." I'd fall apart later.

"Good girl. Now I need something to wrap his leg with." He frowned. "Not his clothes. He needs them to stay warm." He started to pull his shirt off, but I stopped him.

"You're all wet. My shirt is dry under the poncho." I pulled my shirt off with the poncho still on to keep it dry and handed it over. He tore it into wide strips. "Is there anything to use as a splint? It should be splinted."

I'd tripped over small branches coming down the hill. Now I found one of the right length. He took the unused portion of my shirt to wipe it as dry as possible. Then he splinted my father's leg.

My father's eyes went wide with pain, and he held my hand so hard the circulation was cut off. The resulting splint was clumsy but would keep his leg immobilized until a professional could look at it. Then we proceeded to get him out of the car.

I'd not have been able to do it alone. My father was a large man and I'm not large at all, but Jace Browne was as tall as my father, perhaps taller, and had an athletic build that spoke of sports or perhaps a military background and he took my father's full weight while I helped keep him steady. And slowly, carefully, inch by inch, we got him out of the car.

"Now for the hill. You just came down it. Do you know what it's like?"

"It's slippery. Really bad."

He swore under his breath, then took a firmer grip on my father, who was shivering uncontrollably. "We have to get him warm soon." He looked at me through the rain. "Are you up to this? Can you take his other side and hold on if one of us slides?"

I nodded, and we took the first step up the steep incline. The climb was three steps up and two steps sliding back with my father shaking harder as time passed while trying not to cry out in pain each time we slid backwards. I would have cried myself except we were too busy.

When I thought we were doomed to failure, the road appeared, and soon we were next to Jace Browne's SUV. "You open the passenger's door while I hold him."

"Shouldn't he be in the back seat so I can steady him?"

"He needs heat and it'll get warm faster in front." I nodded, and soon my father was in the SUV. Jace Brown buckled him in and then got into the driver's side, while I climbed in behind my father. Jace turned around in the middle of the road, and we headed to town and the hospital as I prayed that my father would be okay until we got there.

As soon as we reached an area with cell service, I called the hospital and told them we were on our way. It was a short distance from there so there was no reason for them to send an ambulance, and Jace Brown got us there as fast as any ambulance could have done and didn't cause another accident in the pouring rain, which said something about his driving skills. The man could have been a race car driver, and I was thankful he'd been nearby when my father's car was run off the road. But I put those thoughts aside as we pulled into the emergency entrance where people in medical garb were waiting with a gurney.

CHAPTER 2

"Thank you for everything," I told Jace Browne several hours later after the doctor said my father's leg was set and explained that he had a concussion, but they didn't think it was serious enough to be kept overnight. So we were free to go. In the middle of the night. "I don't know what I'd have done without you."

I expected him to politely say I was welcome and leave. Instead, he looked at me through slitted eyes and asked, "How, exactly, do you plan on getting home?"

I sagged. "I don't know. I'll think of something."

"I'll take you."

I eyed the clock on the waiting room wall. "I can't ask you to stay longer. You've been here for hours." He hadn't complained or acted as if he was in a hurry. "You must be late for wherever you were headed."

His shoulders lifted. "No place, really, and no particular time to be there."

"You were going no place in a pouring rain?" I wanted to bite my tongue as soon as I spoke because my words were unthinking and too blunt. As usual.

"I'm sorry. It's none of my business, and I'm just glad you were where you were. But you've done so much already. I can't ask more."

"The motels in town are full. I know because I'd have stopped at one if there'd been a vacancy. That's why I kept going, rain or no rain." Which explained how he'd ended up on a country road in a thunderstorm in the middle of the night. "But it was no big deal. If I'd have slept in my car, it wouldn't be the first time. But I'm here now, you don't have a way to get home, I happen to have a car, and I'm at loose ends. So why not? Though a cup of coffee when we get there will be much appreciated."

I checked the clock again. It was past midnight Way past. "We have extra bedrooms. You're welcome to one of them. It's the least we can do."

"That would be wonderful. It's turning out to be a long night."

The downpour had lessened to an all-night rain by the time my father's paperwork was complete and a nurse had wheeled him to the entrance. He was tired but alert and didn't complain as he was helped into the passenger seat of Jace's much-used SUV, though the fact that he accepted help said how traumatic the accident had been. My father didn't let anyone help him. He'd spend his old age throwing things at nurses.

The ride home was quiet, with my father dozing and Jace driving as carefully as during the trip to the hospital, but a lot slower. He knew how to get to where my father had been run off the road but needed directions after that. It was an easy extra mile or so down the road, but he'd have missed our driveway that was hidden by brush and evergreens. And, of course, there was the gate I had to open manually because the remote was in my father's car at the bottom of a ditch.

The gate was followed by the long driveway with numerous turns and twists that ran along a ridge that was acceptable in good weather and couldn't be navigated by even the best of drivers when rain turned the ground into mud. But the rain hadn't yet turned it into a quagmire, and Jace got us to the cabin.

I had to open the garage door manually for the same reason I'd had to open the gate, but the attached garage made getting my father into the house fairly easy. Soon he was in the living room and protesting that he wanted to enjoy coffee with Jace and me, and there was no way we could force him to go to bed until he was good and ready. I figured the pain meds from the hospital were working.

So the three of us had strong, black coffee with tons of cream and sugar and a choice of flavors that turned simple coffee into luxurious treats until we were practically drowned in so much caffeine that we knew we'd not sleep a wink. We decided to stay awake and watch the sun come up if the rain ended and let it peek through. We did stay up till dawn by the clock, but the rain never quit, and we never saw sunshine. Eventually my father reluctantly agreed to go to bed.

I showed Jace a spare bedroom of the several my parents had insisted on being built when we had the cabin remodeled. He brought in a backpack containing his things, and with no sun to wake us up because the rain still fell, we all three slept past noon.

Jace was already in the kitchen when I stumbled there after waking up. He was staring at the top-of-the-line cappuccino machine that took up half of one of the several kitchen counters from that remodel that my father had insisted would make cooking easier for my mother. Of course it didn't because she never cooked. She hated anything cooking related. But I loved the new kitchen. Now a frustrated Jace considered the cappuccino machine. "How does this thing work?"

"Darned if I know," my father said from the doorway, as he appeared with the crutches he'd been given the night before but not used because he'd been too wiped out to even consider looking at them. But we'd brought them in and left them beside his bed.

Now he stared at his favorite nemesis, the cappuccino machine. "It's one of those ridiculous things that's so shiny it'll cause blindness if you look at it too long. It's supposed to do everything and more, and it will if you can figure out how to use it, which you can't because it's too complicated for normal minds to grasp its many functions, so instead you use a real coffee pot to make actual coffee." He used a crutch to point at a cabinet door. "There's one in that cabinet."

Jace failed to hide a grin that he sent my way that

said my father must be recovering nicely, judging by that speech. Then he found the coffee pot we'd used since I was a kid and made coffee, while I scrambled eggs and my father made toast, leaning his brand new crutches against the wall and singing under his breath because, as he explained while the bread toasted, he was still here and kicking after having been in an accident. Plus, the rain was ending, the sun was coming out, and life was good. He was my father again, full-throated and full of life and positivity.

The sunshine, though, was brief. It lasted long enough for us to enjoy breakfast on the deck after wiping the furniture dry. It warmed our bodies nicely, but shortly after bringing our dishes back inside, a new batch of clouds scudded across the sky and turned the world dark once more. "Another storm already?"

My father frowned. "More rain means more mud. The driveway is already bad, another storm will make it deadly and the gravel road beyond the driveway will be every bit as bad. Both will be undriveable." He looked at Jace. "I hope you don't have anywhere to be because you won't make it to the road, let alone to the highway, until the rain ends and the mud dries."

He waved expansively at the cabin that was now many times larger than when I'd been a kid, thanks to that remodel. "As you can see, we have a lot of room. You're welcome to stay as long as you want, and I hope you do because I'd hate for you to die by mudslide after rescuing me and probably saving my life."

Jace's look met mine for a second time, the first being when my father had entered the room and expansively taken charge. He asked silently if my father meant what he was saying. I nodded imperceptibly that he did, indeed, mean every word, as I promised myself that I'd explain further when we were alone. I'd explain how being able to offer things to people was a big deal to my father because he'd not been able to when he was growing up.

My father's eyes narrowed as he watched that private exchange between Jace and me, and I knew he'd also noticed the first one. Now he smiled. He smiled for a long time and didn't try to hide it. We didn't need the sun because that smile was as bright as a sunny day.

What was behind that smile? Why'd two simple glances between two people almost set him dancing and would have if he'd had two good legs?

My father's eyes then slit even more in thought and a look came over his face that no one would recognize except my mother and me, and I only knew what he was thinking because I'd seen it many times during my life.

That smile had something to do with Jace. Something Jace had said. Or done. Or thought. Something that had been triggered by those looks between Jace and me and I had no idea what direction my father's thoughts could possibly take except that it was positive in nature, which I knew because of that smile.

My father watched Jace all that day. Jace had agreed to stay until it was safe to drive. I suspected his decision was made after my father contacted a tow service to have his car towed. He was told that, given the condition of the road, it couldn't be towed any time soon. Next week, maybe.

Jace overheard the phone conversation and his eyes went wide, and once again our looks met as I indicated that, yes, our driveway and the road truly were that bad and my father wasn't exaggerating. And once again, my father noticed Jace and me communicating silently. And once again, he smiled.

That smile said my father wasn't upset about Jace being delayed. Or about the mud. Of course the mud didn't bother my father. He loved it. True isolation was one of the things he loved about the cabin. Guests didn't always feel the same way when they were forced to accept our hospitality longer than planned because of the mud, but my father enjoyed company and was a great host, and they always were reluctant to leave when the driveway finally dried up.

Now I was pretty sure he was glad the tow service wouldn't venture into the area because that meant he didn't have to convince Jace to stay. For some reason he wanted Jace to stay and he was glad the weather and the tow service did the convincing for him, and he was secretly pleased when Jace didn't insist on leaving.

I watched my father and failed to read his mind beyond that he had a plan for Jace, which was usual for him because my father always had plans. They were his life's work and behind the several fortunes he'd made. I had no clue what this current plan might be except that he was totally aware that Jace had possibly saved his life, and so was now a special person in his eyes and deserving of special treatment.

The thing was, Jace was an observant person. He knew my father was watching him, he just didn't know why. I didn't know either but decided that when my father wasn't present it would be my duty to explain my parent to the man who was now being considered for -- something.

That time came hours later as the sun would have slanted towards the treetops if the rain and clouds hadn't obscured it. My father finally, after much argument, had agreed to go back to bed. He was exhausted and needed sleep, though he refused to admit it.

It was Jace who finally talked him into resting, and my father only agreed because the man who'd saved his life should be listened to and because he wanted to be on Jace's good side in order to get Jace to do whatever he wanted him to do. To do whatever was behind that secret smile every time he looked at the man who'd possibly saved his life. So he retired, leaving Jace and me to watch TV and the rain sluicing down the huge, floor-to-ceiling plate-glass windows that took the place of the more normal ones I'd grown up with.

"Nice place," Jace said cautiously as a beginning to

a conversation.

"You can be honest, Jace. It's more than nice. It's huge, for starters, at least as cabins go. Spacious, I believe was the architect's term. And so well designed that all the money and work that went into the remodel isn't obvious. Which is good because I still love it even after it was changed almost out of existence."

He leaned against the back of his chair and chuckled. "Okay. I'll admit it. You said 'cabin' and that's what I expected, so I was a bit surprised by this place when we arrived." His eyebrows drew together. "But not the driveway. It doesn't match the rest of the place. It's awful, and I find that fact intriguing."

I laughed along with him but not so quietly. "When my father sold his first company, he immediately remodeled this cabin and money was no object. It's comfortable and convenient and has everything any of us could ever want. But he loves isolation and the driveway that we fought ever since I was tiny guarantees that only a true hermit would enjoy being here, and there are times when my father qualifies. As do my mom and me. So the driveway wasn't touched. As a result, I'm afraid you're stuck here until the mud dries."

CHAPTER 3

Jace shifted in his chair. "Like I said, I have nowhere in particular to go, and no set schedule to get there."

"But you must have been going somewhere. Otherwise, why be going anywhere at all?"

"I'm recently discharged from the Army and have no plan for the rest of my life. I figured a trip might give me ideas."

"I suspect my father has ideas in that regard. Have you seen the way he watches you?"

"I noticed. Why? Does he think I'm a murderer or something?"

I tried to explain my father. "It's the way he is. How he works. He started a company when I was a tiny kid. Then he sold it and used the money to remodel the cabin and make more money. And so on. He hasn't stopped yet."

"So you are rich?"

"We live well."

"Obviously, but what's that got to do with him

watching me?"

"I honestly don't know, but when he looks at you, he has the same look he always has when he has a new, brilliant idea, and his gut feelings about things are usually spot on. It's what has made him so successful."

He mulled that over. "I guess it doesn't matter why. I'll leave in a day or so."

"No you won't. I know this mud. With all the rain we've had, it'll take a week for it to dry."

"Okay. So I'll stay more than a day or so. I'll enjoy every minute of my time here in this large and very comfortable so-called cabin."

At that moment my father's cell phone rang. I ran to get it because he was asleep, but before I could reach his bedroom, I heard his voice. So I returned to the main room.

Minutes later my father showed up in his pajamas, leaning on those crutches and with the phone still in his hand. He stared at Jace. His face was unreadable except that happy look was gone, replaced by something totally serious. "You look military. Do you know how to handle a rifle?"

"Recent military so, yes, I know how."

My father's face turned even grimmer, if such was possible. "Want a job?"

Jace examined my father and asked carefully and with no expression whatsoever, "What kind of job?"

"The kind that might require using a weapon. I have rifles. They are for hunting but they work by the same principle as those you have experience with."

Jace didn't so much as blink. "What can you tell me about this job?"

"That was my wife on the phone. She says we are in danger. That someone is trying to do us harm."

Jace drew in his breath and expelled it slowly. "Like running you off the road."

My father nodded. "Like that. Or like kidnapping my daughter. There's been a threat. To my daughter, Brynn. To all of us, but to her specifically."

There was silence for a long time as my stomach turned over. All I heard was the ticking of the grandfather clock in a corner that had been there since long before the remodel until Jace asked quietly, "Did she say why someone might do that?"

"My wife is a biologist. An epidemiologist to be precise, and she's in the Amazon now with a co-worker. They've made some cockamamy discovery I don't understand, but evidently it's wonderful and someone wants it badly enough to have threatened her and her friend if they don't give them the formula." He grunted. "My wife doesn't take lightly to people doing that and she told them what they could do with their threat and where they could go."

"And shortly after she said that, someone ran you off the road."

My father nodded. "She's on her way home, but it'll take a while to get here."

"In the meantime, you have rifles and there are

people in this cabin for those rifles to protect." Jace looked around at the huge windows that could be easily broken by anyone who wanted to gain access. "And this place isn't a fortress. You can't do it alone, especially with a broken leg."

"Exactly. Interested?"

There was a pause of a half second before Jace replied. "Sure." He looked at me and our looks met. As had happened several times before. "Why not?"

My father nodded curtly as he noted that once more Jace and I had shared a private thought. "We'll discuss details in the morning. In the meantime, Brynn can show you where the gun cabinet is located and you can choose your weapon." He turned toward his bedroom.

He suddenly looked tired. Weary. Exhausted. As if the accident had finally got to him in spite of his insisting he was okay. He looked like he was on the verge of collapse. "Sleep with it next to you, and make sure you are in the room next to Brynn."

He rubbed a hand across his face. "I hate to dump this in your lap with no more information, but I do need sleep. I'm afraid I'm not recovered completely yet."

"Go to bed. Get lots of sleep." Jace smiled without humor. "I'll take care of things. I'll take care of your daughter."

My father nodded wearily. "Keep my daughter safe."

www.ingramcontent.com/pod-product-compliance
Lightning Source LLC
Chambersburg PA
CBHW060316310726
48976CB00007B/2349